About the Author

I, a single mind and passionate artist.
With promise to
Always do my best, with what I have at the time.
Please journey with me through my writing
I bare all and literally place my life on a line.

Victim of circumstance,
offers, enlightenment of which I hope to bare.
Seek solace in the little things
Such as this song I share.

You'll see my scars,
and nothing to mislay.
However
The strength with in my soul
never be taketh away.

Dedication

I dedicate my book to my wonderful customers. I hope you have received a good tattoo experience from me.

I appreciate your loyalty and patience as I have grown into an individual artist.

To the tattoo artists I have had the pleasure of working alongside, good, bad or indifferent. I sincerely wish you all a flourishing future.

To my true friends, who have picked me up every time I have fallen. Dusting off my shoulders and making sure I always had a tissue and a glass of wine on hand.

To my team, I hope I bring about inspiration.

To the universe, for giving me the courage to write.

And to my mother and father, who are the most incredible parents. I wish I had more time with you.

Thank you all so very much.

www.ArtAngelTattoo.com

Beaudette De Lahaye

ART ANGEL TATTOO
PIERCING THE SURFACE

AUSTIN MACAULEY
PUBLISHERS LTD.

A CIP catalogue record for this title is available from the British Library.

ISBN 9781784557140 (Paperback)
ISBN 9781784557164 (Hardback)

www.austinmacauley.com

First Published (2015)
Austin Macauley Publishers Ltd.
25 Canada Square
Canary Wharf
London
E14 5LQ

Printed and bound in Great Britain

Acknowledgments

First and foremost, I offer my sincerest gratitude to all my customers who have had faith in my artistic capability.

Secondly, I would like to make mention (you all know who you are) to the tattoo artists that have inspired, helped and not hindered my growth.

Thirdly, to my foes as your experiences are from which I have drawn enduring strength.

And to my parents for always believing in me even when I did not.

I would like to thank the illustrators for their image contributions.

Contents

Fears...I mean, foreword

I must admit, I am scared out of wits to share my experiences. Sadly, there are not so many positive stories...I have used a pseudonym for publishing, as I still currently work as an artist and have my own shop. In addition, although I hope for change, I may not see that in my lifetime. Moreover, as I am giving evidence for persecution, I am very nervous about being misinterpreted by hard scrutinisers, that are set in their ways and not open to development. People might fail to see my positive inspirations towards an ever-evolving life. I am certain I will be labelled, bashed, victimised and vilified. I could also be excluded and shunned from the only world I know. The world I love. The world of Tattoo Art.

Nevertheless, for any change that has come about, awareness, understanding and education has been the key. I hope my book opens the readers' minds for the consideration of possibility, growth and much needed change.

I have the best intentions.

Jaimie Diamond

1

Love, love, and love my new tattoo

As a youngster in my primary school days, I was always larger than the other girls at school were. I developed from a girl to a woman at a very early age. This was quite normal in my family and I did not know any different. All the women were heavy set in stature. My chest was larger than all of my peers, including most of the female teachers' chests. In fact, if you added up the total amount of combined chest area at my primary school, and compared the area mass with my chest, I would win by a whole cup size...

In addition, as the kids in my school were uneducated to abnormality, they found it sufficient to tease me about my body oddities. This made me withdraw from school activities, and I felt like an outcast throughout my primary and teenage years. It also spilled over into adulthood. These influencing attributes affected adult decisions I made. Rather than standing up for what I believed in, I have often opted to blend in and not rock the boat. For the mere gain of social acceptance.

Looking back, I do feel that one teacher could assume some responsibility here. As she too came across as eager to be on-board with the majority of her students, rather than setting an example. She would hone in on me when I was trying to inconspicuously disappear. When the focus wasn't on me at gym training, I would try to be invisible or sneak off to the bathroom before participating. The sneaking off was to go put on another couple of bras before the sporting activity session. By strapping down my chest and layering my over shoulder boulder holders, I could manage to engage in some sports and activities. My teacher, rather than letting me go and do that; would single me out and question me, until I was as red as a tomato with embarrassment... Seriously, what twelve year old has the 'stones or gumption' to stand up in front of their class peers and say, "Yes Miss, I'd like to take five minutes to throw on a couple bras to hold down my boobs. Then I can run about like all the other kids". At my age now, as an adult, sure no problem, but I did not have the confidence then as a child.

I did not know whether to dread or welcome high school. You hear of initiation stories and goings on of when you first start high school that is intent on scaring you. I was more concerned with another three years of being the school 'odd ball'. I did not think I could cope with being so vastly

4

different. Thankfully, there were other developed girls and odd balls in college and this made me blend in amongst the other students. If you are thinking that the years of primary to high school is longer than three years, you're right. Where I grew up, you have the option to leave at 16, and that is exactly what I did.

My circle of friends during my college years were not the best choice, they were older and college drop outs. They did not attend university and did nothing with their time after they had finished their time at college. I always thought that they could not quite cut the strings from college and make the transition into adulthood, or should I say, assume adult responsibilities. That was why they let people like me hang with them, to continue that connection to college somehow. I saw them for who they were, but loved them all the same. They were my friends and I did not have a whole lot to choose from. They did not tease me and they did not seem to care that I was slightly large in the chest, or a little odd... In fact, I'm sure a couple of the older boys liked my oddity.

A couple of my older friends had tattoos and I admired them. The tattoos on my friends looked great and being artistic myself, I designed a couple I thought I might like to get. My parents were not opposed to the idea of me acquiring a tattoo, they had grown more open minded over the years. We had all lived through a myriad of 'levelling' life events. The ordeals, although some unpleasant, had given us unity, strength, communication and honesty in our family unit. I did not understand this so much when I was younger. Now that I am older, I understand and value their way of parenting.

I was honoured that my parents had given me consent to get one of the tattoos that I had designed for myself. My Father was going to join me and get one as well. So, for my birthday, we booked in and I was allowed to get a small tattoo with the proviso that it was in an area that I could easily cover.

After counting down for many weeks and suppressing my excitement, the day had finally come. It was time for me to get my tattoo.

I walked into a staircase off one of the main streets in town. It was dark stair well and seemed to go on forever. At the top, was a room probably the size of a large living room. A reception counter, creating a seated waiting area on one side and a tattoo area on the other, divided the room. We were spot on with time. My father had severed in the military and punctuality was drilled into me at a young age. I have no complaint as this serves me well today, it is a good attribute to have. We were on time and ready, the tattoo shop smelled weird, it was a clean alcohol, disinfectant smell, crossed with cigarette smoke, and to my amazement, Marijuana. This did not faze me at all, as I had no expectation or knowledge of the experience. I went in and stood by the counter to alert the artist that I was here. The gruff man on the other side, who had not shaved or maybe bathed in weeks, grunted at me to sit down.... Containing my excitement, I did as we were told.

It must have been an hour or so...maybe half an hour that felt like an hour. The gruff looking man was doing something with the tattoo machines and we kept hearing an occasional 'buzz' from the machine. Every time I heard it, I would have a tizzy of butterflies in my tummy. I was so nervous, but super excited at the same time. I had my tattoo design ready, I had drawn, re-drawn, sized and bought copies in case we needed more than one. I couldn't wait and it didn't matter how much pain I was about to undergo. I was getting my tattoo!

Finally, the man grunted again, I didn't know what he said and walked up to the counter, explaining that I had made an appointment and was here for my tattoo. My dad was also here to consent and he was going to get one as well. The gruff looking tattoo man asked what I wanted and I gave him my design. I then had to sit down again, and after a few minutes, I was summoned to his area of the room.

Everything happened quickly; he drew my tattoo on me and then got his machine out. I was sat on this rickety old chair and had one foot in the air and the other on the ground. Not the most glamorous of postures and I was thankful my dad was with me. The machine buzzed and I held on to the chair, I was expecting huge pain! However, it was more of a scratchy, burning sensation. The time seemed to go very fast and I am not sure how long the tattoo took. Once it was finished, I was told to stand up and have a look.

I looked down at my new tattoo and fell madly in love with it. The first part of my body I actually loved! I love, love, loved my new tattoo.

Over the next few weeks I drew and planned my next tattoo. My parents asked me to wait for a while and get used to my first. They did not mind as long as I considered my future and that I may need to hide my tattoo, depending what career path I took. Six months later, I was back for another. During this tattoo, I was far more relaxed as I knew what to expect. The admiration and seeing the perfect images permanently added on my odd body seemed to grow. I loved that one as well and just wanted to get more...

2
You ruined my back!

I was hooked, and on my third tattoo, I was a little over-indulgent. I had designed it five times the size of my other two tattoos. My parents asked me to wait a year, and if I still wanted to get then, they would consent and I could go and get it.

I waited and did exactly as I was asked; I saved up $500.00 and booked it in with a different tattoo studio. I had heard some bad things and did not like how the gruff looking tattoo man came across during my second tattoo with him. I wanted to change the colour of the rose that I was getting from red to blue. Blue is my favourite colour and he said, "No. It is going to be a red rose." I felt too intimidated to argue. So, I have a red rose now.

I found another tattoo shop; this one looked lovely with a glass shop front. Not any ally way with a dark stair case. It was large, light and airy. The whole layout was different and there were many designs to peruse. The shop smelt clean with no smokey smells. I was greeted by a younger person, who had a fair bit or tattoo artwork on himself. I loved the way he looked. He wore his tattoos well. I felt shy and slightly attracted toward him. I showed him my design and told him I had two small ones done already. He took my design and showed it to a woman; she also sported a fair bit of ink and looked great with it. She was a little frosty and did not engage in any conversation with me. I thought this because she was already working on some one's tattoo and was busy. She was looking at me, as if I annoyed her. To break the sharp stare, I piped up and said, "I drew it myself". I did not know what I was thinking...Deep down I was hoping that she might say, *"Good girl, it's a nice tattoo design"*. Or, maybe, *"Would you like to do some designs for us"*?

She ignored me and summonsed the young man serving me. He came back to me after a few minutes and said it would cost $450 dollars. I agreed and he informed me that he would be a few minutes getting everything ready.

It is quite funny how life works out. I know who that lady artist is today, and now that I am a tattoo artist myself, I have promised myself that I will never project that egotistical conduct to any client who is paying me to perform a tattoo for them. As she did to me!

The nice looking guy asked me to come into the tattoo area. He made a stencil and placed it on my back, where I wanted the tattoo situated. He was a little shaky and did not talk to me, at all...He was trembling, to the extent that I had to try and make conversation with him, to soothe my nerves and his. This was a big tattoo and I was nervous again, as if it was my first time. I felt like I was being a problem, so I stopped talking, and didn't want to bother him. I rather wanted to leave and maybe find somewhere else. I wasn't confident in his ability and his quivering made me more nervous. *"Maybe I should just go back to the other guy and get my dad to come with me..."* There was no time. The guy was going to start my tattoo. I didn't want to be a problem, so I didn't say anything.

Heck! What am I doing, this tattoo hurts like crazy... I was knelt on top of a table, over my knees, to stretch my lower back. Similar to a foetal position. This was not the most comfortable position to be in. My legs were going numb, my tummy hurt from kneeling and my boobs hurt from kneeling also. I know good ol' big jugs'. The tattoo really hurt compared to the other times, I thought I was going to die...

I asked if I could have a break after, it must have been two hours. I decide to call a friend to come and pick up me and my car. I did not fancy having to drive home after my tattoo. I still had a fair bit of time to go before finishing. In addition, I had just gained my full license and the drive back home was about 40 minutes out of town. I felt too out of sorts to drive. For some reason, I was finding this tattoo to be very sore. I had eaten before coming to the tattoo shop and bought a sugary drink with me. I had been advised of the instructions on getting my first tattoo and as this tattoo was so much larger. So, I followed the directions a hundred percent.

The guy tattooing me told me we had to keep going, and as soon as I had organised a friend to come get my car and I, we carried on. I had asked my friend to come in two hours, as we had not done very much at this stage. This also worried me a little.

By the time they arrived, I was in agony. My body was cold and my legs were numb, I had been kneeling for 4 hours, with one break in between. I didn't know if I could sit through much more and now that I was not alone. I had the courage to ask how long there was to go. The unsavoury lady scoffed at me and answered that it takes as long as it takes. Again, I did not want to be an unaccommodating customer. After the fifth hour, I burst into tears; my whole body was shaking and I could not control it. I asked to use the bathroom and could barely walk when I stood. I told my friend that it wasn't right, that it hurt really badly. I persevered for another 20 minutes. I couldn't stop crying (I wasn't dramatic or crying loudly, I just could not stop my tears from rolling down my face). My friends had talked to the lady, asking if everything was accurate. They also informed her that I wanted to stop for today. She grabbed a book of crazy piercings, opened it on a picture page of a madly pierced penis, and stuck it in front of my face...I guess the book was to take my mind of the pain. I could not move my hands as I was kneeling again. Therefore, this picture and the odd-looking pierced penis was etching into my brain... *"Awesome, I couldn't feel a single bit of pain after that! A breakthrough in medical research. How about we issue every pain patient there is a pierced penis picture?"*

Finally, the tattoo guy stopped. I did not care how good he looked with his tattoos now; I was in so much pain. I could not see the tattoo very well as the area was bleeding a lot. I handed over my cash, which was now $500 dollars, and not the $450 that I was originally quoted. I was told to purchase some baby care cream and apply that over my tattoo. I asked if they had a little I could take home. As the chemist was not open until the next morning, they did not, and I felt like I had done them an injustice by asking.

I could not sit down in the car; I had to lean over the back seat facing the tailgate. I think some of my muscles had pulled a little bit and it was hard to stretch back into a normal position. My friends offered me a bourbon and cola, I would normally say no in case the alcohol affected my tattoo. I was in so much pain, however, I accepted it gratefully. It was the best bourbon and cola I have ever tasted!

I asked to be dropped off at my parents for the night, my mother helped me clean my tattoo from the bleeding. I was completely drained from the whole nightmare. So, after I cleaned the tattoo, I went to bed. The next morning, I woke up, still in the same position. I had knelt down, half on my bed and half off, my knees on the floor and my body lying on the bed. Stretching my back and in a similar position to how I was when I was being tattooed. This seemed to be the most comfortable position possible. The muscles in my back seemed to be pulled and felt worse when I stretched out or stood up straight. I fell asleep and woke up in the morning in that same position. My knees were white and crazy cold, it took a few minutes to be able to walk and get the blood circulating again. My back had developed a huge scab over the tattooed area. You know, like when you take the skin off your knee by falling on gravel and that thick carpet scab forms. A hard crust forms over the wound and when you bend your knee it splits open and feels awful...A scab exactly like that had formed on my back, over my tattoo. My mum called the tattoo shop to see what needed to be done and to ask them if this was a normal occurrence. I guessed it was too early to be calling, as there was no answer at the tattoo shop. I went to the doctor and he could not advise me either. Just to keep the area clean and covered. Back then, tattooing was still not as acceptable as it is today; there was no generic information about how to look after your tattoo and you couldn't jump on to Google and find out either.

We did go to the chemist and purchased a mild antiseptic cream and some gauze to cover the area. I soaked, cleaned and applied the new gauze each day, hoping that my tattoo would be okay. I had to have antibiotics and time off work. Sitting and sleeping was also a difficult task, whilst my tattoo healed. My tattoo experience had put a lid on the pot and I had no desire to get anymore tattoos for a few years.

3
My Tattoo Apprenticeship

I ended up going to another artist a few years later to have the entire tattoo on my back redone. It took two separate sessions to fix. Just to make the tattoo look presentable. There is now some scarring and areas of the tattoo that are raised and bumpy. I keep it covered up most of the time. All in all, I give the whole experience a big thumbs down. Only half a star for this tattoo shop.

I have always loved drawing; it gives me a sense of peace and calm. I had designed my own tattoos and had been asked to design artwork for my friends on many occasions. I did not know whether my tattoo designs were any good, in comparison to professional artists who worked in tattoo shops. Besides, no one in the tattoo shops I had visited had given me any feedback. I still loved my tattoos, and although I had had a bad experience, with my last tattoo. The tattoos made me love my imperfect body; and that outweighed all the pain.

I wanted more tattoos and had heard of a new shop in the city that had a great reputation. I drew another design and now that I was older, I wanted my tattoo in a more prominent position. When I went to the shop with my tattoo design, the owner had a look and pointed out a couple of areas that he wanted to modify. He explained why and made comments that my design was good, but needed some changes. This made me feel at ease straight away as he had taken the time to educate me to why alterations needed to be made to my design. How the ink sits in the skin and relaxes, making the smaller details blend out. The basic line width, once healed in the skin, is different to the line width of ballpoint pen on paper. He modified the design and gave me a quote. I booked my tattoo in and had the best tattoo experience ever...The tattoo acquiring candle had been re-lit and was burning brightly.

A few years passed and getting a tattoo on my birthday had become my routine gift to myself. I gained knowledge of the tattoo industry along the way, purely by having a common interest. Especially as I had to consider what I wanted to do with my life, and customer service in a clothing store did not really cut the mustard as a long-term career choice for me.

I had drawn many tattoo designs and decided to take them into a couple of tattoo shops. I was using a pro-active approach to hopefully getting an apprenticeship or feedback on my artwork. I was given the opportunity to join a renowned tattoo shop in the city and my little career began...

On my first day, I was so nervous but excited at the same time. I was aiming to be one of the best artists. I was going to have tons of work and have customers come in and ask specifically for me! I'd made a few contacts already and had gained a small interest and following in my artwork. I felt fantastic and that my life as a tattoo artist had just begun! This was all my dreams coming true and I was finally going to be accepted as a tattoo artist.

I had many grandiose ideas over the next few years and little did I know my first and regular customer in the tattoo industry was going to be...Mr Mop!

As an apprentice, you start out at the bottom, I knew of this. But didn't really know what apprenticing as a tattooist would be like. I didn't mind so much and cleaning did not bother me. I actually had fun, playing music and getting the tasks done before and after the shops opened. Mr Mop and I were an item for some time, while I learnt the ins and outs of cleaning a tattoo shop. Understanding the importance of combating cross contamination in our industry is hugely relevant. Coming from a strict military background, cleaning, keeping house and high standard levels were already ingrained in me.

Tangibly performing a tattoo looked very simple, transferring designs on to the skin and following the lines... However, there was a whole lot to learn about performing tattoos. And when I did my apprenticeship, there was a lot more to know than there is in this day and age. Today, we have advanced technology and online purchasing of every item you could possibly need to perform a tattoo.

During my apprenticeship, we did not have that luxury. I had to learn all areas of the tattoo trade. We made our own needles. We would clean off the needle bar of its existing needles, group the new set of surgical needles using a jig and re-solder them onto the bar. You had to set the quantity of needles onto the needle bar, grouping them according to what outcome you wanted to achieve when tattooing. When I started making needles, the requirements were just numbers and groupings, for example, a five round or a seven flat. I had to make about 30 – 50 needles each week, sterilise, autoclave and then label them for use. They would take me days to make when I first started out...and if they we not correctly assembled, I would get them back and told to redo them. This was all unpaid work. Attending an apprenticeship in the tattoo industry is unpaid. You work your way up and, eventually, you will receive a percentage for the tattoos that you perform.

Understanding how to make good needle sets fell in to place for me when I started tattooing. I could relate to what line size the piece of tattoo artwork needed and make the needle grouping as required. I found that relative training techniques work better for me.

This varies greatly amongst artists; we all use different needle groupings and clusters based on the artwork style we aim to achieve. And I was very grateful when the day came for me to pass up making needles for the other artists. The artists I worked with were a fickle bunch and depending what mood they were in, determined how many needles I would actually have to re-make. I cared about what I was doing and never took a laid-back approach. I was quite hurt when I started getting my needles back and told to re-stencil designs. I would also be told off for not having their table set up them way they wanted it... And heaven forbid if I was to get their coffee or lunches orders wrong!

I nearly quit a couple of times and my boss told me that was what they wanted. Other artists want you to quit during your apprenticeship, especially if you show artistic potential... I never grasped this, I wanted to do a good job and if I did my job well as an apprentice, surely it helped the other artists. I maintained a positive attitude and the more I grew in my abilities as a tattoo artist, the stroppier the behaviour from my fellow co-workers became.

4

Hop, skip and a jump

My boss was diagnosed with a health issue and it did not help that he was an avid alcoholic. I have been around people that could drink and on a regular basis, but a 10am wine is for the hardened drinker, that is for sure. We tried to help, and help him manage his shop, but bills were not being paid, material was not being ordered and artists eventually dropped off. His priorities had shifted and he was losing his shop. My boss was always good to me; I honestly felt like he really cared about my goals and believed that I could turn into a great tattoo artist.

He had some contacts and organised for me to go and work in a neighbouring country. I was sent over to a small northern shop that had potential for me to grow. I thought all my Christmases had come at once. Not only was my apprenticeship almost over, but the shop needed me to step up and be one of its main artists.

When I got there, I understood why. I was the only tattoo artist, as the other tattooists had left. Again, I did not mind, as I found the constant fight for work amongst the other artists a little draining. And the fact that I did not have to fight for a good tattoo piece was a relief. I did not ask why the other artists had left and still was of the apprentice mind-set that it was none of my business.

The shop owner was a woman in her late forties. She was a no-nonsense kind of woman, small but...scary. She specialised in piercing and I was to perform the tattoo art for her at her tattoo shop. *"That's okay... I can make this work,"* I thought to myself.

My boss was a stern lady, I thought that may have been a first impression. Maybe to make sure I wouldn't give her any trouble. There was a completely different reason, and when I came to know her a little better, I understood why. She had good reason for be hardened and I was to come to understand that. In fact, the longer I am in the industry, the more I find myself following in her footsteps; Toughening and becoming cautious.

The boss lady barked at me mostly and I chalked it up to her approach. I did not like her mannerisms, but considered it her way. I considered I should toughen up, weather the rain and not let it bother me. However, that did not last too long and, one day, I told her what I thought. I had lost my cool and shouted back at her. The day had been long and her constant barking had worn me down. She took me out for a drink and seemed to be more tolerable in her approach toward me after that day. I always wanted to know why she was so harsh. I don't have to work there with her; it is a job after all. If she did not like me as an artist, I would be happy to leave her shop. I was aware and understood my status and position in the tattoo industry. I know I would have found it extremely hard to find a shop that would take me on as a contracting tattoo artist. I was still fresh, as I had just come out of my apprenticeship time period. But I didn't want to be at a shop where I constantly felt like I was doing wrong. I told her this, and she made it very clear that I would not get work anywhere else. I believed her and figured I would just do my job...

The boss lady had a boyish haircut, deep set dark eyes that were cold even when she laughed. There was no trust or love left in her...none at all!

I did not know anything about the tattoo industry, or how the bikers had the monopoly over the tattoo shops. If I had, I would have never pursued becoming a tattoo artist as a career.

The boss lady told me that her and her partner opened the shop together. When they opened, there were only a couple of tattoo shops in the town. Apparently, her partner belonged to a motorbike riders' club. This club was an innocent club in comparison to the 'bikers' clubs that are renowned in this country. The town had not been bothered by any biker ownership, but some of the adjacent towns had. Her tattoo shop was new and they were doing well in business as a couple. I am not sure of the specifics, but after they opened the tattoo shop, they started receiving royalty and payment orders. This is where you are required to pay a weekly percentage for protection money, or allowance money, to one of the bikers associations. This percentage may range from $500 dollars per week to $2000 +, it was dependent on your business earnings. This will allow you to trade in the service of tattooing in that town. They will then provide protection against other bikers, or gangs, that also try to claim the ownership or payment from you. And if you didn't agree, the bikers would forcefully stop you from trading. This was similar behaviour to what the mobsters used to do.

My boss lady claimed her husband had been shot dead and her children were sent to her family, who lived out of state. I was a little sceptical about the story and was not sure if I believed it. She was left to continue running the shop and paying monetary percentages. This was also the reason why her artists had left. Her husband was a tattoo artist and they had a couple of other men who also worked with him.

The shop needed a tattoo artist, and when my old boss called his contacts in the area, I was appointed to go and work in her shop. A young tattooist and the perfect candidate...

I made a few friends in this town and spoke to a couple of long term locals. You do not talk about some of the goings on. People who know about that side of life are generally spooked. And those that don't, have no consideration for it.

Apparently, she was to keep the shop open and pay weekly amounts to guys who came in. In the beginning, I did not see or notice the bikers coming in for collection. So many people came in and out of the shop and I was insanely busy. I enjoyed being the main tattoo artist and getting to perform many different tattoos.

After a while, I cottoned on to regular patched bikers that came in around every two weeks.

I recognised them, but never spoke to them. Anyway, they never tried talking to me. I knew my place and the whole concept of the matter scared me.

I did not want to believe the boss lady's story. The more I thought about it, the more I resented my subscription to working there. I felt like a factory ant, and my boss lady worked me hard! I was on a thirty five percent rate for each tattoo I performed. The novelty of working alone wore off quickly. I missed talking to the other artists. Another factor that stood out to me was I was the only artist in the tattoo shop. It was a very presentable tattoo shop as well. Tattoo shops normally have two or three competent artists and an apprentice, minimum. I had just come out of my apprenticeship. She had no other artists working for her and no-one seemed interested to work at that shop either. There was absolutely no interest in the two years that I had worked there.

Time passed and I kept working, I knew I had to put in lots of time and effort to become a good tattoo artist and that is what I intended to do. I missed my parents and friends, but other than that, I lived and breathed to perform tattoos. I figured you have to make the necessary scarifies to exceed in life.

I didn't comprehend exactly what I would be expected to sacrifice...

5
I was that girl on but a
different plane

One New Year, I arranged to fly home to see my family.
Flying at that time of year was very popular, so I organised
a night deal that was slightly cheaper. Those late night flight
deals generally have fewer passengers. Which is great, as
sometimes you do not have to share seating and you can
spread out. There was hardly anyone on the flight and I had

a whole row to myself...Great news. I relaxed and tried to nap lightly. I didn't want to be tired and was looked forward to seeing my parents.

Whilst I was on the plane, there was a girl about my age four rows in front of me. She was in the middle section of seating in the centre of the plane. I could see she also had two chairs to herself and could spread herself over them both. Being located behind her, on the left side, I had a clear view diagonally. Not that I was watching her. She just stood out to me and I couldn't help but notice oddities. The flight attendants seem to check on her more often. As though there was a problem. She did not fuss, nor want anything they offered during their rounds of the plane. She did little to engage with anyone and looked dishevelled and pale. I had a very chilling feeling about her, for some reason. I overheard one of the flight attendants say to another attendant that she was flying home to attend a funeral. My heart felt heavy for her, but somewhat odd. Like I knew her in some way, or was attached to her somehow...

Seeing my parents was moving. I love my parents so much. I am a lucky lady to have had such decent and loving parents such as mine. I was picked up from the airport and we celebrated the remainder of New Year's Eve with close friends, who had gathered for a small party at my parents' home. The evening was fantastic and New Year's Day was off to a nice start. We had breakfast and then I shot off to see some friends that I hadn't seen for almost two years. Everyone was pleased to see me, but I still had an odd feeling in the pit of my stomach. There was something going on, I was sure. A couple of days later, I came back to my parents' house after visiting. I found my mum and her sister in the lounge. My mum was in a made bed, which had not been there two days prior, before I left to visit friends. It was the afternoon, I just assumed they were having a 'duvet day' and watching movies. We did that sometimes on rainy days, so I thought nothing of it. I opened the lounge door and asked if anyone wanted a hot drink.

I was asked to come in and sit down, as they had something to tell me. My mum was near to tears, and from that moment, I knew I was about to receive some bad news. My mother had been diagnosed with a bad form of cancer and was not expected to live longer than a few years. Looking back, my family gave me the best positive information. On the bright side, we were all full of hope that mum would beat this. My friends and family had rallied around in support of treatments to combat the illness. I was caught up in the hope. Too caught up to consider anything else. Nevertheless, the future did not look the best.

I had to fly back to work and inform my boss. I decided to finish and go home to support my mother. I wanted to do right by everyone and finish any outstanding tattoo work, so

I did not leave her in the lurch with customers at the tattoo shop. I did believe her story and did not want to leave her or let her down. I knew that she would be without a tattoo artist and may not be able to find one so easily. I had formed a small connection with her also, and respectfully, I wanted her to understand that there were some honourable people in this world; Me, hopefully, being one of them. I told her that I would give her two months' notice, before leaving to go back home. I was very booked up with clientele and wanted to give her enough time to at least advertise for another tattoo artist. I would stay a maximum of two months, unless my mother took a turn for the worse.

When I told her, she showed no emotion whatsoever...I was in tears, my mother had taken a turn for the worse and the doctor had diagnosed a six month life term. I could not fathom losing my mother and the reality had set in. She accused me of lying to leave her shop. I was so devastated by her response. Looking back now, I should have left then and there. But I wanted to do the right by her and felt bad.

The time went by so slowly and I felt like a walking shell, completely numb. I felt nothing inside of me, no pain, no excitement...nothing. If I drank alcohol, I would not feel the euphoria that I used to, that buzz that I would normally get off of a couple of drinks. Even if I drank a lot, I would just pass out and wake up in the morning. The meaning or reason for being at that shop had left me. I started to resent her and her tattoo shop. I could not take working there and knowing I was on borrowed time with my mother at home. I could clearly see my boss lady's antics to manipulate me. She would say some cruel things to me, suggesting that I should harden up and trivialised my suffering by telling me that everyone loses people...That I should just focus on the work and that my parents were not in my life anyway, as I had chosen to work in a different country. Maybe she was right, maybe I had deserted my family for my career. I only ever wanted to make something of myself, so my parents would be proud of me. Everything was so cloudy and confusing during this time and I did not trust her one bit. To be fair, I suspected she may try to stop me from leaving to go back home...

I was right; I started noticing the same cars coincidentally everywhere I went. Not just similar cars, the same number plates. I was being followed. I would turn up to the bar and the same few patched people were there. I noticed certain cars parked across the road from my house. Dark tinted cars right at the bottom of my driveway. They weren't even trying to be inconspicuous. Everything felt weird and I was getting a little paranoid.

I reached out and spoke to a friend about it. Shane knew my flat mates and was a tattooist for the other shop in town. He helped me tune my tattoo machines. Talking to him was how I found out that the other tattoo artist I had previously worked with had put me wrong with tattoo machine tunings. He spent time with me, explaining the components and different tattoo machine set ups. He also checked my machines after I tuned myself them to make sure I had set them up correctly.

Everyone in my flat were fans of the Band 'Pantera' and I met Shane at a 'Farewell Dime' party. When Dime-bag Darryl was shot on stage, my whole flat was rocked with the loss. They threw a frenzied party, where the only band that was played all night was the legendary Pantera. Shane liked them so much, he tattooed the logo on his calf muscle. I liked Pantera very much too and could not comprehend what had gone down. I superficially claimed that without 'Pantera' there would be no more Phil Anselmo. He was the lead singer of the band and my ultimate man candy.

When I spoke to Shane, he had already heard that I would be leaving soon; I broke down and cried my eyes out. He consoled me, but he could not be seen to be helping me. He had his own boss. His boss also had connections and knew my boss. A couple of days later, my flatmates told me that he been sent away; they told me he said to tell me to fly home as soon as I was able. I was not sure what to believe or what was happening. This whole existence, knowledge... tribulation, whatever, seemed so dreamlike. I went to see his mom; I met her, when Shane helped me tune my tattoo machines. He had an outside garage, where he worked on his equipment. There was loads of different tools and a rugged table made out of crates and wood. I remember being spooked at the rickety old shed and all the cobwebs that were around. It was hard to absorb what Shane was trying to teach me, when I was concerned that one of the spiders that made the cobwebs may come out to visit us. His mom informed me he had gone to another state and did not really give me any time. She had been really nice when I first met her. I think I may have created some trouble for Shane, I hoped I had not.

What was going on? I was not used to this chessboard-manipulated movement. I did not know about gangs or bikers, other than to stay away from them! I called my boss and went to talk to her, I asked her outright. *"What's going on?"* She said she had received a note under her shop door from my old boss's connections. It was from a well-known tattooist, who had arranged my job originally with her shop. The note said, "*I need to stop mucking around and do my job*" and it was signed by the tattooist. Who might I add was also a president of an area bike gang.

I actually felt sick to my stomach. This was not normality to me. I had not subscribed to being labelled in alignment with a gang or biker group. To be dictated to about what I could earn, whom I could be friends with and when I could travel home...I was an artist; I did not do anything to draw unwanted attention to myself. I had just worked damn hard for the last couple of years, for her and in her shop.

I knew inside I had to leave, but not advertise the fact. I had to keep it quiet, and that is what I did. Over the next two days, I organised my flights. Packed my most important belongings and left everything else behind. I packed discreetly, so nothing looked removed from my room, as I was not sure whom I could trust. My boss lady had stopped into my flat with a trivial matter; she had never stopped by before, so I wondered if she suspected that I would flee. My flatmates knew her also and I did not want to take any chances, so I did not tell them. They felt awkward about how Shane had been sent away. I figured that they blamed me.

I went to work the next day, knowing I had a flight for that evening. I booked a very late light plane to one of the major cities and organised the main flight from there. I booked it from the next town just in case my boss called and checked the flights. After a gruelling long day, I went home after work as normal; the parked cars were there again at the end of the drive as usual. They stayed there until around 9pm. Once they had left, I called a taxi. I grabbed my suitcase and paid the driver up front to drive to the next town. It cost around two hundred and fifty dollars.

My heart was beating so badly, I had such a horrible feeling. The whole day I felt as though I would burst.

34

We got to the tiny airport; I was to take a plane that had about 11 miners on it to the closest city. Then take a main flight to home. My flight was booked for 3am. I did not know what time I would be able to leave and needed to plan for the taxi trip to the next town. When I arrived at the airport I had a couple of hours to wait, and although I was still scared, I felt slightly relieved being surrounded by mine working people and flight crew.

Finally, I was on a plane home. I did not call my parents until I arrived at the airport. I was worried that I would not get home and I did not want to concern them any more than I had to. My dad came to collect me. It dawned on me, when I was on the plane looking pale and dishevelled, like death warmed up, that the flight attendants seem to check on me. I didn't want anything they offered during their rounds and did little to engage with anyone. That odd familiar feeling I had about the grieving girl on the plane the last time I went home.

It was I, I was that girl, but on this plane...

6
My own tattoo shop

I stood around and watched my friends, family and foes. Drink, eat and be social. They were here to celebrate the opening of my own tattoo shop. As I gazed around, I should have felt fortunate and happy.

As a tattoo artist, you gain a lot of friends and acquaintances. I loved the popularity at first, it was a breath of fresh air compared to my teenage years. But, now the popularity seemed superficial and more of a chore. And when the friendship is challenged, as you often find at crunch time, when you asked for help and your so-called friends are not interested.

I wanted some help from my friends, but when I asked a lot of them were suddenly too busy.

Don't get me wrong, I am lucky enough to have a handful of remarkable friends. If I had asked them, they would have helped me. I was wrong to expect help from the hangers-on. In fact, I was wrong to consider these types of people my actual friends. Every tattoo shop and studio has the 'hang on group' that occupies the shop as their social hang out. Most of the time, they Tweet and Instagram positive statements about the shop, amongst their friends. This is great for networking and promotions. However, when it comes time to 'work' time and enforcing the services provided by the tattoo shop as a priority over the hanging-out, the communication can be undesirably received. In circumstances I have encountered, some of the non-friends actually take offence. Not wanting to offend anyone and being new to business, the last desire I had was to create unwanted attention. This is one of the small, seemingly frustrating, attributes of owning a tattoo shop, as I found out.

So, my friends and foes drank their fill and lost their dignities. No one let me down in that area. Including family members, who were also under the influence, provided a spectacular display of drama. Leaving me with a 'grand' opening, or should I say, a huge mess.

Note to self, *"Next time, do not have a shop opening at your newly refurbished tattoo shop."*

I had saved money working three jobs, requiring a small loan and put into operation all the fit out and set up myself. Only hiring trades men when necessary. This should have been a really positive part of my life, however, instead, I found it to be really hard.

I blamed my distant feelings and emotions on the grief related to the death of my mother. And the ordeal in trying to leave the tattoo shop where I had worked. I was keeping busy, but when I paused to stop for a moment, I felt as though I would have an out of body experience. Looking out and not really being a part of life. My circumstances were weighing on me. I felt as though I could drift out of my body, float around and see people and situations unambiguously for what and who they were. Almost as if I had gained a sixth sense.

I had lost my ability to look on the optimistic side and lost my patience for insensitive people. It was if I could see lucidly and was more conscious. I was bound by friends and family and felt that they all had a want, advantage or agenda... Nothing seemed true or actual. Again, I chalked this up to my heartache.

I threw myself into my tattoo shop wholeheartedly. My point of difference for my tattoo shop was to be my client service. Using the distasteful experiences of my past when acquiring my tattoos and turning them into a positive. A motivation to deliver a higher level of tattoo service and standards.

I sought solace in the small attributes of the tattoo service. I made sure I was on time and ready for the customer. If they were booked in at 10am, I was ready to start with them at 10am. I had worked with artists that would have two to three cigarettes, grunt, set up and organise their designs, whilst the customer was there waiting for their appointment. This meant the poor customer had sat there for 30 minutes to an hour, while the artist got himself or herself organised. This seemed to be a normality in tattoo shops I had worked in. I wanted my tattoo shop to be different.

I had previously prearranged the customer's design, so most of the work would have been done by the time they arrived for their tattoo appointment. I also made design forms that detailed the information I needed, so I could prepare for their tattoo session accurately. Customers would complete this when they made a booking. I found this a great process for effective time management. I organised after care cream and aftercare information sheets for when they had received their new tattoo. No one was to be sent home without aftercare, or endure the experiences that I had done previously.

I had set prices and implemented the correct health license for my tattoo shop. Where I lived, the council regulations around Tattoo and Body Piercing were relaxed, there are areas on the city outskirts, where you could argue that you fell under the neighbouring town. And those towns had different or no regulations in place for tattoo shops. Most of the other studios used this excuse. Also, nearly all tattoo shops worked in cash only. I personally never carried too much cash with me and felt that other customers should have the option. I also felt that it injected a level of professionalism by having a bank card payment system in place in my tattoo shop. This also worked well when someone paid a deposit, I could give them a receipt chit stapled to their booking card. My intention was to provide good customer service in my tattoo shop, tailoring tattoo designs to what the customer wanted.

I was open a couple of weeks and doing very well, to my surprise. I was expecting some visitations from industry connections and maybe some biker gang members. I had done my homework and set up my small personalised tattoo shop in an area that would not impact any other tattoo business. I also planned to explain to any gang members that felt I should pay them, that I didn't not subscribe to their expectation and that I respected them for whom they were, but had no interest in any affiliation. I thought, if I could make them understand that I was a small, insignificant tattoo shop, that I loved my job more than making vast amounts of money, then they may leave me alone.

I was wrong! I possibly need to explain to you, the reader, in more detail here. I would say a huge percentage, not a few, but MOST shops are if not owned, then expected to pay fees to certain area biker gangs. You can check the statistics by 'Googling' the area and gang-owned tattoo shops...The statistics are far lower than the reality. And it is extremely hard to get hard evidence to support the claim that they are connected. Some gangs will run drugs through tattoo shops also. As soon as you succumb to their involvement, you are caught in their web.

Two weeks after I had opened the tattoo shop, pressure from local gangs presented itself. The first was chit-chat through the grape vine. The hanger-on friends would inform me of any speculation or rumours. The rumour was that my new tattoo shop was targeted to be burned down. I was a little unnerved by this and went and spoke to the local Police Department. I also took some business cards with me and wanted the police to know that my motivation was to provide a good customer service in my tattoo shop. A few days later, I had a post-it note stuck to my shop window in the morning, "*Close or will burn down shop*". I discarded it, as the police had informed me that it would merely be a scare tactic.

When I set up my tattoo shop, I had to buy furnishings and chattels. Setting up the tattoo shop on a budget, meant I had to purchase a lot of second hand or pre-used furniture. Only my tattoo equipment was new. So, I wasn't too worried if my shop did get burned down. I had full insurance, and if the ordeal came about, I would set up a new shop and have the luxury of purchasing new furnishings rather than secondhand ones. A silver lining maybe that made me feel more at ease about the situation. I made this known to my 'friends' and hoped it travelled back, maybe diffusing the shop burning threats.

I lived about a ten minute driving distance from my tattoo shop, in traffic; So, not too far. I left my home around 8.40am each morning, as I enjoyed arriving in to the shop early. I loved making sure that everything was perfect, and when my first customer for the day walked in, the shop was presented amazingly. I had mounted a small T.V on the wall for customers to watch during their tattoo and not so heavy rock music played throughout my shop. It was clean and well-presented. I hoped my tattoo shop made a great impression and created a desirable ambiance. I took pleasure in the presentation and service of my new tattoo shop. These were great feelings to experience after feeling so discontented.

A week after the finding the note stuck on my tattoo shop door, I had a visit to my home. It happened, as I was sorting out my morning. I watched an older style Japanese, white, utility van park in front of my house. I lived in a cul-de-sac street and my house was situated in the bend of the street. The van pulled up and stopped abruptly and two very scruffy looking work men jumped out of the van, wearing high visibility jackets. They came to my door and I opened it, leaving the fly screen door closed and locked. They were shuffling nervously and didn't come too close to the door as if to make a quick exit. As I opened the door, one of the men blurted out information to me. I didn't hear him clearly, but understood that I was being instructed to move and close my shop. And having the men come to my home informed me that they knew who I was and where I lived...They then turned and got back in the van quickly. I didn't get to hear the threat to quote it, I could hardly understand them, but I thought I did recognise one of the men.

I grew up and lived in this small town, I went to the nearby college and know most people in the town. Some of the teenagers I went to school with have parents who own businesses in the area. The town's size and intimacy was the main reason as to why I chose to open my tattoo shop there. I had small rapport already with school peers and their parents. Anyone who knew me and my parents, knew I had good ethics and was raised well. I went to see my friend after work, I was reluctant to go back to the police. Although they had been polite, I was made to feel as if I was wasting their time with my tattoo shop fire threats. I also didn't have any evidence of relevant information for them. My friend's father had a local business that had been open for years and he was well known. I spoke to him and described the man I thought I had seen. Sure enough, the van was one of the local excavating companies and my friend's dad knew who had visited me. My friend's dad told me not to worry and that I wouldn't hear from them again. I did not go to the police, but looking back, I should have done. It was not the thing to do in my town and in hindsight, if I had my time again, I would have.

7

"Mickey" Blue Eyes

I didn't get any problems after that and the next six months or so were good at my small tattoo shop. I had met someone and the two combined was a perfect distraction from the 'broken' life I knew.

I met Kevin during my first year in business; he had the most beautiful blue eyes I had ever seen. I swore he could see right into my soul with them. He came into my tattoo shop to check things out and enquired about some tattoo work. He had some work done, and in a few months, we were seeing each other. He had recently moved back to town from overseas with his two daughters. After living overseas for the last ten years, he thought it was time to come home. He had extended family here and had been through a rough break up with his ex-partner from overseas. He was 38 years of age with two teenage daughters. I was hesitant before entering any relationship and his baggage did set off some alarm bells. So, I was a little bit concerned, but not in any rush for major commitment. I did consider that I had left 'love' too long and men my age were either coupled up, having had or just starting to have children. Being an older man, I hoped he had a broader perspective on life and a healthy level of intellect. Also, with him having children, there would be no pressure on me to have children. I just opened my shop, and although I see children in my future, I was nowhere near ready. I decided I was prepared to give the relationship a go, but wanted to take the whole enchilada one bite at time, with no haste.

Full-on involvement with him had suddenly been forced upon me. Kevin had come off of his motorcycle and was injured badly. His teenage daughters were left with his friends. His friends were men, who you wouldn't want your grandmother left with, let alone two young beautiful naive teenager girls....He didn't have too many people around and I felt like I couldn't abandon him. This is another choice I would change if I could. I made myself available to help him, and felt that if the role was reversed, that someone would help me. I have that ingrained for some reason, to help others and in return, heaven forbid, that I need help, it would be returned. This is a great area to point out expectations. I expect that I would be given help, if ever presented with the circumstances, as I am helping others; Maybe that's a flaw in my behaviour.

Kevin was released from hospital and the next four weeks or so flew by. I was busy managing work and trying to help him out. He was constantly in a lot of pain, and after a few weeks of not making much recovery, I pressed Kevin to go back to the doctors. The findings were surprising, he had broken both arms, not just the one, and fractured his foot. Only one broken arm was diagnosed by the hospital he attended, when he fell off of his motorbike.

Now, he was almost covered in casts from head to foot, but he still didn't seem to be on the mend. A few more weeks passed and I would say that his health was deteriorating. He had developed a greyish tone to his skin and was losing weight. He was a big man anyway and carried some weight, but was healthy with it. I had noticed his appetite had changed and he had started to look gaunt in the face.

On Sundays, I worked by appointment only. Giving me the freedom to have a day off, occasionally. This Sunday, I had a clear day. After work on the Saturday evening, I had planned to go to Kevin's house and stay; this had become regular occurrence. I text messaged ahead and asked what everyone wanted for dinner. I shut the tattoo shop and headed to the supermarket. Kevin lived up north, about an hour drive from the shop, if using the motorway. When I got there, he was looking awfully pale and rubbing his stomach on one side. I made dinner and we settled in for a night of movies. One of his girls was going to attend a party and we expected her to be back later that night. As we watched the movie, I could see something wasn't quite right with Kevin. I was going to get him back to the hospital in the morning, but didn't bother to tell him of my intention. He was a typical man and didn't like attending doctors' surgeries or hospitals. I had learned it was best to tackle the idea in the moment. So, I would suggest the idea when I wanted him to actually get in the car and go. Otherwise, it wouldn't happen.

4am and I was wide awake, Kevin's breathing had been laboured all night and he kept letting out little moans, he also seemed somewhat non-comprehensive all evening. In my fatigue from the day, I considered that maybe I was worrying too much, and that was why I left the decision to head back to the hospital until the morning. At 4.20am, I had had enough. I woke him up and told him to get in the car. I used a manner that he knew I was not arguing or messing around. He didn't argue either, and that was when I knew something was not quite right with him. By the time we left, the sun was due to rise. I had warmed the car up and had a blanket set up to keep him warm. I was very aware, driving down the motorway, that Kevin was in pain. For some reason, I had a very bad feeling.

It was as if all odds were against getting him to the hospital. His daughter hadn't come home as promised. His other daughter threw a tantrum when asked her to stay back and wait for her sister; A big commotion for that hour of the morning.

Then, bang! *"You must be joking"...* A flat tyre on the motorway.

"Someone doesn't want this man to get better" I thought. The light from the sun was just coming up and I had to fumble around in the car's trunk and find the car jack and tyre iron... We had taken his old junky car, as it was parked outside. I had parked mine in the garage, as I had the food shopping and it was easier to bring up the bags from the internally accessible garage. *"Why didn't I take my car"?*

Thank goodness there was a spare tyre. I changed the flat tyre and then carried on down motorway toward the hospital. When we got to the hospital, we had to wait in the waiting room for a couple of hours. I bothered the receptionist a few times and she said we could go over to the other private doctor's facility and we could get an assessment earlier than waiting. We would have to pay for that service, whereas, if we continued waiting in the public hospital, the visit would be free. Cost didn't factor in at this stage, he needed to see someone urgently. This was early Sunday morning, and being the main hospital for the town, they were busy after the Saturday evenings casualties. I decided to take Kevin over to the other private doctors for an assessment.

We were there ten minutes and had an appointment instantly. It cost $100, but was well worth the money. I would have gone there straight away, if I had known about the service. The doctor examined him and sent us straight back to the emergency part of the main hospital, informing us that we would be met and taken through for further examinations, straight away...I explained to the doctor that Kevin had come off of his bike 7 weeks prior and had broken limbs, some of which had not been found out about until recently.

We were met and he was whisked off to another room. I was allowed to go through and wait outside his examination room. He was then given a bed and dressed in a gown. We were placed in a corridor with other patients awaiting results, as the Saturday evening had been full of patient admissions. I suspected something not so good was wrong with Kevin, as his hospital bed had a sign that said, "nil by mouth". That meant that something was wrong, and they may want to operate shortly. I waited with him until 3pm that Sunday, and then left to go and make sure his daughters were okay. I promised to be back in the morning at 8am, which was the earliest visiting time.

His daughter that had gone out parting had not come home, by the time I had arrived back at Kevin's house. And the other daughter, who had thrown a paddy, was now in despair. To top it all off, she had called one of Kevin's mates, rather than calling me or him. And you guessed it, the most childlike friend Kevin could possibly have was also there. I made a game plan to look for the daughter who had not come home and called all of the friends in her sister's cell phone list. I also went to the police station and asked for advice. I sent Kevin's mate to a couple of addresses to speak to the parents, in case the teens were not telling the truth...It turned out I was right to have and we found the delinquent daughter up at her friends', apparently if dad could have a girlfriend then she could have a boyfriend! *"Aw heck... just what I need right now."* I thought this might be more or less related to her dad coming off the bike, rather than having a girlfriend. I wasn't really around much before the accident. We had only dated a few times. Anyway, I explained where her dad was and gave her the option of staying with me closer to the hospital, or with Kevin's mate at her home. I intended to visit him in the morning and then come back to his house in the afternoon. She wanted to stay at her boyfriend's house and I made it clear that this was not an option. Her father was not here to allow it, so she would come back to the house. I even had to threaten calling the police to get her back home. I gave the other daughter the option as well, and she wanted to come and stay with me. I departed with the paddy-throwing daughter, and left the delinquent daughter with Kevin's mate. I made it very clear to Kevin's mate, that if anything happens to her, I'd cut his bits and pieces off...There was a reason why I hadn't dated for so long, trust in amorous men was something I lacked. And there was only one way to communicate with this kind of man. I had no intention of carrying out any action described in my threat, but I needed him to think that I possibly may consider the action. He was a simple man and I made sure our communications were simple and crystal clear.

8am, bright and early, the paddy-throwing daughter and I waited to see Kevin. Even though she was not my child, and although she had been a magnanimous brat, I couldn't help caring for her. I checked on her during the evening. He had such beautiful children. She slept soundly at my home. Both his girls had such a rough time with their relocation, their father's bike accident and now this dilemma. *"Gosh, they should be off partying and doing fun stuff, being teenagers"*. My heart did go out to them both.

We went to the hospital and I was informed that Kevin was going into surgery at 10am. They were prepping him now and we should come back in the late afternoon. They were going to call me every step of the way. I took the little one for some breakfast and then to work. She was a little darling and helped me with some odd cleaning jobs. I called my customers and cleared my next two days. I figured that would give me enough time to make a game plan about how to manage with Kevin's children. Their mother was never spoken about, and after losing mine, I didn't push for any information. I figured they would let me know in good time...We were not their yet in the relationship. I really had just been on a few dates with him.

At 11am, we had a call from the hospital to say Kevin had been through surgery and we could come in around 2pm. When we went to the hospital, I asked about the time, as we had been informed that the surgery was to be at 11? I was informed that Kevin had passed into unconsciousness and they had to operate on him straight away. I still wasn't sure what was wrong with him...2pm came and went and we were moved from one waiting room to another, still waiting to see him. I spoke to the one of the doctors and was informed he had been taken back into surgery, and we should come back around 5pm.

I decided to go and collect Kevin's other daughter and his friend and bring them down to the hospital. I thought this might not end well, and the least I could do was get them all to the hospital to see their dad!

At 8pm, we were able to see Kevin. We were in a sectioned off area of the intensive care unit. Visitors were only allowed in one by one, and we all had to wear abominable snowman outfits to eliminate contamination. His girls were devastated, I was tired and numb, Kevin's mate was also devastated..."*And yes, Kevin's mate made it three teenagers*".

He had a punctured lung that was slowly deteriorating and not functioning. It collapsed that morning and again that afternoon. Undiagnosed and all caused by the bike accident he had a few weeks earlier. He would be in hospital for a little while. At 10pm, he had seen everyone. His girls were exhausted and I decided to take everyone back to his house for some rest. I had some unexpected goings on crop-up during the time at the hospital. I was tired and I needed some sleep to get my head around the information I had been presented with...

During the evening, I had a call from overseas on my cell phone. A lady claiming to be Kevin's partner and the mother of his son. She said she had to get my phone number off of my business website and demanded to know what was going on. Why I hadn't called her and clued-up the other children?

I told her, I had the girls with me and didn't know of any other family; That the girls intended to call everyone that would be concerned the following morning. I promised to personally call her and update her every day, until Kevin was well enough to call her himself. She had told me there were five kids! *"Five kids and I learned he was 43 years of age, not 38 as he had lead me to believe. How stupid was I?"*

Kevin and his motorcycle were on the mend.

8

A 'hit' ordered on my own tattoo shop

I had relocated my tattoo shop after a year, as the lease had a demolition clause included in it. I wasn't financially stable enough to be able to move premise on a short period of notice, which was the expectation of the clause. I moved closer to the city and took on a road frontage shop. It was more expensive, but a good location for a small business. I had done some homework on the area and made sure there was no other tattoo studios in that area. Making sure I wouldn't be treading on anyone's toes, yet again.

One morning, while I was working on a tattoo in the newly located shop, my piercer was minding the front desk. A man came in and requested to know who owned the tattoo shop. Lisa, my piercer, asked who he was, and he informed her that he was a police officer, following up a credit card fraud notice. This didn't faze her as we had people from all walks of life come into the tattoo shop. She asked him for ID and told him that the fraud was not likely to be related to us, as we did not accept credit cards. Only bank card transactions using the customers checking or savings accounts. He left straight away, which was very odd, leaving no details or explanation. Lisa informed me about him when my customer stopped to have a cigarette break.

I was working on a large tattoo piece that morning and my customer would have been with me for around three hours. Shortly after the break, Lisa came to interrupt me and let me know that there were now actual police officers at the reception desk. They were demanding to see the owner of the tattoo shop instantly. I politely excused myself and went out to the front of the tattoo shop, where the reception desk was located. I was shown identification badges by two officers dressed in plain clothing and was asked to speak with them in private. I asked my customer if he minded having another cigarette outside the shop for 5 minutes.

I didn't need Lisa to leave, and had nothing to hide. I was of the impression that the police were at my tattoo shop by mistake.

They asked if I knew Kevin, and who owned the tattoo shop. I claimed that I had been seeing Kevin for around 7 months and this was my tattoo shop. The policemen demanded I called Kevin, who was working in a neighbouring town, for them. They requested I instruct him to meet me at that town's police station straight away. I did and he agreed. They told me to close the shop immediately, and send my staff and customers home. They asked me to come down the coffee shop, five doors down from my tattoo shop. I was instructed to walk in and buy a coffee and then walk to my car. Not to look for them, or give off any knowledge that I knew they were waiting for me. I was not to engage with them in any way publicly. They would wait for me, follow me to my car and then follow me in an undercover police car to the neighbouring town's police station. This was where I was to meet up with Kevin. The police would then inform me of what the concerns were. I started to shake and didn't know what was going on...

I asked Lisa to leave the tattoo shop and that I would call her to let her know when we could resume work. Frantically, I placed a note on the wall and closed the shop, apologising to my customers and giving him a free sitting for his inconvenience. This was something out of the movies. I couldn't believe what was happening, the whole event felt bizarre. I did as I was told, bought a coffee, trying not to shake, when it was passed to me and went straight to my car. As soon as I was in my car, I locked the doors...silly, but it was an instant reaction. I drove onto the main highway and continued toward the police station in the neighbouring town. I did notice a car behind me, but couldn't concentrate on the road and them at the same time. I was coming up to a police car parked on the breakdown lane of the motorway, and as I approached him, he moved off in front of me and flashed for me to follow him. I did so, all the way to the Police station.

At the police station, I met up with Kevin and was very distressed. I wasn't happy about having to close my shop or that I had no information as to what was 'going on'. They took us both into the back area of the police station. I had never even been in this area before. The only times I had been to a station was to apply for my driver's license and enquire for help about the burn threats made to my tattoo shop. We were both questioned about the tattoo shop ownership and informed that a local gang had placed a 'hit' out on two addresses. 1. My tattoo shop. 2. My family's home address. They apparently wanted to seize Kevin's motorcycle and destroy the tattoo shop. I was horrified. *"What"???*

We were then split up and questioned separately. I felt shocked and then angry. I had just been through so much with this liar of a man and I didn't know how much more I could take. I had no reason for any of this, so I blamed him. And the fact that they had my family's address made my blood boil. Right at that point in time, I concluded that this man was definitely not worth my family's, or my own, well-being!

After being questioned and pouring out the honest truth about everything I could have possible done to provoke this, I was informed that we would have to evacuate my family from their home. I must commend the police at this point, they had spent the day questioning us both. They had been very patient and sympathetic to me. They talked to me, so I understood the importance of what was happening and advised me accordingly. They had organised a car to follow me back to my parents' house and a separate car to follow Kevin to pick up his daughters from their house. They had organised a hotel, where we were all to stay for the next two days.

I arrived outside my family's house, tailed by a police car. Can you imagine? My father had spent his whole life in a professional environment. I, his loving daughter, is now on his doorstep, having to explain that he needs to pack his bags and leave his home.

Dad opened the door and humbly greeted the police officers and I. I briefly explained the circumstances. He packed a bag and came with me to the hotel. Again, we were accompanied by the police car. I was so embarrassed for my family. I was trying to live my life in the correct way, conforming and being an esteemed member of society. I respected values and wanted to be recognised as a successful business owner in the town. I had partied in my twenties, but now I was older and had high expectations for myself. I could not believe this was happening and felt ashamed for my family.

I stayed with my family in the hotel room; Kevin and his daughters had the next room. There was a door between the two rooms and we could pass through into each other rooms. That evening, I stayed with my family and didn't really want to spend any time with Kevin. The police didn't provide any solid information, only that we had to spend the next two nights at the hotel. We were told not to drive around and not to go home. There would be a police officer attending the hotel in the morning around 9.30am.

My father had lost his cool by the morning, he had to call his boss at work and explain why he wouldn't be able to attend work that day or the next. And that he couldn't provide a date at this stage as to when he could resume work...My dad is a very clever man and was used to being head of the family, so the lack of information and the embarrassment he faced calling his boss was not good.

The next morning, there was more questioning. The police kept Kevin and I divided. My family and I stayed together and Kevin was on his own. His daughters were not questioned and sent to watch television in another room. We found out that Kevin's last name was not his real name, that it had been changed, around ten years ago, when he had to go and live in another country. He had been involved with a biker gang and some form of business deal. He was the target, but had no residential address that could be linked to him. That was why they targeted my shop and my families address. That was fuelled by me owning an independent tattoo shop. We weren't given any more information other than that. We were told that it would be best to go away for a while. That the police had undercover agents that would try and diffuse the situation.

So, as advised, we all went and stayed away for a week. We had to sign documents that stopped any correspondence or claims about the events that had happened. As the police operations may be compromised if any information was to get out. This was all a bit much. My family and I did not have the financial luxury of taking weeks off work. I stood to lose my shop if I could not meet my expenditures, and by being closed, I was losing customers, let alone not being operational.

I decided I was going to return to work and open the shop again. I asked the police about the safety of the public in my shop and they told me it was my risk. They did assure me that it is unlikely that anything would happen now, but did not make a certain secure statements. I had moved in with Kevin by this time, to help with his recovery and shorten the driving distance between the shop and the two houses.

Once we returned home, I moved out as soon as I could afford to. We had a fiscal venture in the planning, but there was no trust. The relationship between us went downhill rapidly. I could not trust him, or anything he told me.

Also, he had planned to move his partner, the mother of his son, to town from overseas. This meant he was playing me and her for weeks. I ended everything.

We had a car and a little money in a financial venture, as my name was on everything, I was the one responsible for accumulating costs, etc. We had some costs come up and I had to sell the car, close the business deal and rent a room rather than a whole flat. I had financially and personally invested in this man, without stopping to consider anything. *"How stupid have I been"?* Every event happened so fast, with no me time in between. Flatting was now the only option I had. If I took on more costs than I could handle at that time, I ran the risk of losing my tattoo shop...I still had to recover from being closed suddenly, with no explanation, and in a small town, news of business closures happen fast. I had made some majorly stupid decisions, they were all based on my current circumstances. I didn't even get to decide if I liked this man, or if we were compatible on any level. I just did what I knew to do which was work and keep house...I was so furious at myself. I cared for everybody and I should not have!

9
Fundraiser or fun eraser?

I explained to the police, that a while back, a bike club that claimed to be a riding group only had helped me put on a function to raise money for a little girl. An acquaintance's daughter was diagnosed with leukaemia and it was incurable. Sadly, once she had been tested, the little girl had a time limit placed on her life. This pulled on my heart strings and I felt her anguish.

I knew her mother from the tattoo and piecing industry. She was heavily tattooed, had piercings and very brightly coloured hair. She dressed in a punk style and looked very alternative compared to most mums in the town. She was a popular girl, slightly heavy set and very tall. She stood out and would dominate the entire crowd by her appearance. I admired her character and thought the genre very 'suicide girl'. She had a confidence but gave off a shy demeanour. I thought it was a well-rehearsed performance. *"How on earth could you have the confidence to sport the dress style in public as she did and be shy"?*

Anyhow, she looked like something out of a fashion magazine or heavy music video; it looked good and supported the tattoo and piercing industry. We had the tattoo interest in common and became friends for a while. I knew her daughter and had babysat her a couple of times. I grew to disparage the mother and had the perspective that her priorities were a lot to be desired. It was bought to my attention that her daughter was terminally ill, and although I didn't have much respect for the mother, I still believed that it would be one of the worst things any person could endure. Having lost my mother made me feel strongly about loss of life, as a whole.

The news was brought to my attention by a mutual school teacher friend. The school and community had declined helping the little girl financially, due to the mother's carry on and guise. This was a conversation for huge debate. I would like to point out that people who have tattoos and an alternative lifestyle are not bad parents. Although often deemed so by others who share a different way of life. However, you always find that the minority let down the majority. By people who choose to place their persona and visual upkeep as a priority above and beyond the welfare of their child. Understandably, this gives good cause for the debate. I know many colourful and tattooed people, whom are perfect parents. Parents who inspire me; I hope to have a child myself someday.

However, I can see the other side and when the finances are limited, I believe in making sure your daughter is in a nice and warm room at night and this actuality is a far higher priority than the latest fashion or bright new hair colour.

No one in the town was prepared to organise a fundraising event. And although I would have rather ignored it, I felt compelled to help. Also, I had the connections and resources to pull together a fundraiser with a little bit of time and effort. And that is what I did for the sick little girl.

Anyhow, I did. I was in contact with one of Kevin's friends, who was in a riding group. This group was specifically not a gang, and a family oriented group, or so they claimed. I met with their front-runner to propose and event. The event would portray them in an optimistic light in the community and in turn, help a little girl; simple. I explained that I wanted to open the event to hot-rods, cars and the tattoo scene. This would attract more people whom I had networks with and shift the focus from the biker aspect of the event. The riding group was on board with that idea. They had a bar and a licensed premise. They would provide the fundraiser location, as well as organising the car and bike cruise. I organised and paid for the, bands, food, and advertising; Making sure that I worked closely with one of their members, getting consent and sign off along the way.

I informed the little girl's mother and made sure she would be okay with this and introduced her to all the parties. She was thankful and the hospital let her bring her daughter to the event for presentation of the raised money.

We had a great response and a large turnout. Everyone donated and some of my tattoo clients donated up to $100 each. That evening, the monies were totalled. I was on the gate, as I knew most of the people attending. I was greeting everyone and thanking them for their attendance. The cruise went well and there was a poker run for the riders. I had given tattoo shop vouchers and T-shirts for prizes. The bike group also kicked in some left over prizes from old rallies.

All in all, the day was great! I had a huge day and was relieved when one of the club members took the float and wanted to sort out the totals...I wanted to have a drink and take some good photos of the event. I had been doing a basic money count during the day and figured we definitely had raised $4000 dollars easily. I'd made a list of names of people who donated above $50 dollars, to thank them publicly at prize giving as well. I asked the club if I could do this prior to them presenting the money, when I handed the float over. They said sure, no problem. The club made a big 'dummy' cheque to present and had placed the little girl's name on the title of the cheque.

When it came time for the presentation, I was not given any chance to thank anyone as I hoped. The little girl and her family had arrived and the cheque was presented for $2800.00 dollars. My heart sank. Those bloody boys had skimmed the fundraiser proceeds. I had a list of names that added to just under that amount. I was actually expecting closer to $5000.00 and I bet that is why I wasn't allowed to say thank you and list the names of everyone who had donated over $50.00 dollars. The amounts would add up and be inconsistent with the presented amount...I was hugely disappointed.

Two weeks went by and I thought no more of it. I was very let down and decided never to organise any function with another biker group again. How could all these men who have nice bikes and leathers keep the fundraising proceeds? There was nothing I could do and I decided to leave things at that.

I had a visit from the little girl's mother after a few weeks and apparently the biker club had not transferred any money at all. They had promised to do so over the first week after the fundraiser event, and I had assumed they had done so. I thought that there must have been a misunderstanding. As the girl's mother did not know the biker group, I agreed to follow up on the money and its whereabouts.

I called the biker member that I was to be working with and asked about the money. I knew this guy before he was a biker and he appeared to generally be a nice guy. He also had a daughter, so I knew this cause pulled on his heart strings also. I left the query with him.

A week later, I had assumed that the bikers had cleared up the non-payment. I had not heard from anyone and had thought the matter resolved. It came to light that nothing had been solved, when a TV company that featured consumers that had been ripped-off called me. They claimed I had used the event as publicity, that my tattoo shop had presented the fundraising event alongside the biker group. That the money was raised and kept, and that was absolutely despicable! I understood and clarified my position in the fundraiser. I had names, emails, photos and receipts to back up my claim. And the necessary evidence to make the story factual and publishable. The TV people came and spoke with me and I asked for a mediation outside of the public view. I provided names and contact details of everyone I had been dealing with to help aid the resolution of the matter.

This placed the little girl and her mum in an awful situation, above and beyond the predicament that they were already in. I wasn't hugely economic and was able to pay two instalments of $600.00 to them. I did this of my own free will and couldn't fathom the how appalling this fundraiser had turned out to be.

The biker group had come up with lots of different excuses as to why they did not want to make the payment to the sick little girl's mother. Apparently, the father of the child had contacted them and demanded that he be paid the money. They claimed that I had not specified who the money had to be given to. There was no contract and they were happy to provide some food stamps and a wig for the sick girl. They claimed that the mother would use the money for tattoos and drugs. One of their members worked for a wig company. They used the mother's alternative lifestyle and accused me and her family of being tattooed drug users. Apparently, this wasn't the first time they had conducted a fundraiser and then pocketed the proceeds. Biker menaces getting away with tricking society again.

I had organised the flyers, my tattoo shop had presented the small fundraising event at the biker's location. I had photos of a 'dummy cheque' being handed to the family and a list of donators. When I called the club on behalf of the mother, I was told that the club didn't want anything to do with me.

They had pocketed every cent of the raised money. The TV show was meant to help mediate a remedy, but the biker group was too strong and had a very good lawyer advising them of what to do and say.

Meanwhile, the little girl was dying and didn't receive any financial aid apart from what I could afford. And I didn't have much, I had no more to give than what I gave.

The little angel died 6 months later and I attended the funeral. Not one member from the biker club did. "*I am so sorry I couldn't do more for you, little one. So sorry!*"

So, I explained this to the police and I believed it was me whom they were targeting with the hit on my tattoo shop. I had stood up to these biker thugs and would continue to do so...

The police ensured me that this was not the case. They were aware of the story I had regaled and that had nothing to do with this particular incident. I gave them all the details and information I had.

10
I'd been played good and proper

I had grown close to one of Kevin's friends, prior to our break up. He seemed to notice the effort I constantly put into Kevin and his family, whereas Kevin did not. Both Kevin and Martin wanted to do something more career and business based. They had approached me about combining a bar, pool hall and entertainment centre, that would house my tattoo shop. I would lease space and set up my tattoo shop and art gallery, and they would run the other areas. My shop was about 3 years old now and I was doing okay. I was open to the idea, but not sold on it. There was a lot of crucial foundation work and planning that had to happen first. They were both very persistent with wanting me involved. To start, I didn't understand why I was needed for the venture. As it turned out, I was only one who had a credit rating and who could obtain a lease on a building.

I wasn't sure about the idea, but open to the concept. I have always thought many hands make light work and this might be worthwhile, if planned correctly. I figured everyone could show their sincerity with the venture and proposed that each individual deposit $800.00 into a combined bank account. This combined money would be used to set up the concept, project plan and company shareholder details. As a first step, I made it clear that I would only consider the project if all foundations and planning was done in the beginning. I intended to use the finances we had combined for a lawyer and official business set up costs. If that wasn't acceptable, I didn't want to be a part of the project. We opened an account and I placed $800 into it, Martin placed $300 and Kevin, nothing. That pretty much said it all and the project didn't progress forward from there.

I found Kevin's friend Martin quite good to talk too. He was a very lovely looking man, with olive skin and the 'V' frame. He had big shoulders, built up from manual labour. With distinguished features and dark hair, he looked good and was more athletic than Kevin. His charm and charisma didn't occur to me while I was committed to Kevin. In fact, they didn't occur to me for a while. The magic moments of realising someone of the opposite sex was attractive, looks good, has a nice smile or smelt good hadn't registered with me. For a long time, I had been walking around in a desensitised body. Missing some of life's momentous details.

Martin had been at mine and Kevin's home a few times for dinner, and he had witnessed Kevin's girls during their chronic brat phase. One night was particularly trying, and Kevin never did anything in my defence. Again, I chalked it up to the girls having been through such a turbulent time recently. That evening, Martin came into the kitchen and said he'd never treat me like that. I smiled, shrugged it off and thought nothing of it. I thought he was making a comment to ease the situation.

Kevin and I were on borrowed time. I had no trust in him and lacked patience with his demanding daughters. The care and consideration that I had for the girls had been rapidly plummeting, I almost had nothing more to give. I was working longer hours, ignoring the house necessities and chores. I had backed off from participating in anything with the whole family. We were over. It was just a matter of time. As soon a house share came up close to work, I intended to lease it and moved out.

I found a place and moved. Finally! A few weeks went by and my world seemed less turbulent. I had more time to myself and had taken up walking on a daily basis. We had some woodland walks close to the house and I thoroughly enjoyed 'my time'.

I thought my life may be too good to be true, and sure enough, the mayhem started again. I can only assume that Kevin had realised how good he had had things when I was with him. I started getting phone calls with no answer on both the shop and my cell phone. The caller identity was blocked, so I could not find out who had made the call. I had my car window smashed and my shopping taken out of the car. I parked in a multi-storey car park and was hopeful that they had cameras. I enquired and they didn't, which was a shame.

I arrived at work one morning and my tattoo shop door was sealed closed by the sealing glue that Kevin uses. Also, the locks had been glued so I could not open the door. I had a note under the door to give him the car. I thought all this a bit 'silly' when you consider what we had gone through with the 'hit' a few weeks prior. I went straight to the police and they issued a trespass notice on both the shop and my new home address. I hadn't given Kevin my new address and wanted to keep it from the documentation. I had also written to him with my plan of closing our accounts and paying off our accrued debt with the car sale. And that I would also split the remaining amount with him equally. I had the car away being fixed from the window smash, and was also having it valeted, so I could take it to an auction. It was an older car and the type that costs an arm and a leg financially to repair. I wanted to sell it fast, before I had to spend any more money on it.

I lived about a 10 minute walk to work, so I didn't need a car straight away. I anticipated getting everything straightened out and then look at buying a nice professional looking car for my tattoo shop. The car sold, I closed and paid off everything that connect the two of us, and then split the difference. I gave the cash to Martin, as Kevin couldn't come to the tattoo shop. I had kept all the receipts and provided Kevin a copy of all my actions to show him I hadn't kept anything I shouldn't have. I was hoping this would diffuse the animosity Kevin had toward me. You guessed it. It didn't.

Over the next two months I received threats via text message. I had bought a car and had my shop logo stuck on it as a sticker. I parked it in the multi-story car park and found it with the door handles sealed up. Then the locks were closed with glue. Then, I found it with the mirrors smashed. This was one night after the next, after the next...I decided to leave the car at home most of the time and only use it when I had to buy bulk stock for the tattoo shop. The car usage wasn't systematic; sometimes, I would only leave the car in the car park for a couple of hours. I was surprised at how Kevin knew of my movements. I ignored everything for a while, hoping it would ease off. Looking back now, I can see the connection. The scare tactics were occurring to push me closer to Martin. And Martin was so conveniently there when those occurrences happened. Very silly me!

Martin called by to the shop a couple of times. I didn't really know why, as he didn't want to book in for a tattoo. We exchanged phone numbers and text messaged each other for a while. I honestly thought he was actually being considerate and cared about me; That he was making sure that I was okay considering the dreadful time I was having with Kevin. I knew the goings on were Kevin's doing, as I knew of the cheap glues and sealers he used for his work.

They matched what was on my car and shop door. It was also convenient that the note had been placed under the door and that the door had been sealed up shut. I had grown a strong belief that Kevin had a very unsavoury past and considered that Martin knew of it. They had been friends for only a couple of years, but knew of each other, or that is what they claimed.

One night, Martin came to my house to console me. I was upset due to Kevin's constant harassment. I had a protection order granted immediately on Kevin, but it did no good. I was amazed at how fast I received one. The paper of the order was comforting, but did absolutely nothing to stop him. My car and shop was vandalised, I would have him park across my car in the mall car park, so I couldn't back out, and he would leave just before the police arrived. I received one hundred and forty dollars' worth of pizzas delivered to my home one evening, I found that quite funny. I don't eat pizza, and wouldn't order one let alone fifty odd. I was more worried now, as Kevin now had my home address. He must have followed me home after work that evening. I was only home 20 minutes and the door rang with the delivery of a load of pizzas. I didn't trust him. And although I could defend myself if he physically tried to hurt me, as he had come off of his bike and had a lung collapse earlier in the year, I was still frightened of what he could do and why he was carrying on the way he was. In my mind, I had readied myself to hurt him in his weak areas, if he cornered me unexpectedly. I left the car at home now and walked to and from work every day. My insurance only covered the first three incidents and I didn't want to continue making claims and paying higher fees. His so-called friends caused me more concern. The money oriented drop kicks...They'd do anything, and I mean anything, for a buck!

Martin stayed for a few hours and then left. He started coming over on a regular basis, his timing was impeccable. He always knew when Kevin had done something. Martin had also gained a connection with my father; they both rode and shared a beer on occasion. Supposedly, he was looking out for my welfare. Looking back, I can see very clearly and I get angry with myself for being so gullible. They had set it up. I was too much of an asset to let go of. I think I was so pre-occupied with the tattoo shop, the ordeal with the police and the sick little girl. I didn't take a step back and look at what was really going on. I didn't ask if it was possible that there could be an agenda. Or maybe I didn't want to see the truth?

I had some major wounds and couldn't quite make head nor tail of anything, I seemed to be making the wrong decisions; one after the other after the other. My lease was coming to an end and I was questioning whether to keep the shop open, or relocate to somewhere less costly. I opted for relocating as the tattoo shop was my only form of income, and I figured I should try to work smarter not harder.

I found a place that had an apartment, that I could live in as well as work from. By consolidating rental and utility bills, I considered this to be a financially smart option.

I had built up some debt from relocating and premise regulation compliance. I had experienced such a disorderly time and must admit that my life choices did not reflect well on my tattoo shop. The visitations from patched member had started up again. They would just come into my shop and look around. I had accepted this to be a part of the daily grind. I had noticed one particular aspect, however. Only one biker gang would come in, different members each time, but the same biker gang and I hadn't been visited by them before.

11

New location, new start and a clean slate

I had moved to a new location. Not only was this shop cheaper, but it also had a two bedroom small apartment above it. I thought this would be perfect, I could consolidate the business and accommodation costs. This was a fresh start and clean slate.

Martin was visiting quite frequently and stayed over many times. I wouldn't have said that we had developed into a full term relationship, as I hadn't realised I had subscribed to that... But he did visit me very often, even without an invite. I think we may have had a difference of opinion here. This was my error completely for not making the boundaries clear. He came over so often, when he told me he had to move out of his house and suggested moving in with me, as we were a couple, I was slightly taken a back. I thought about the proposal and could see his point of view, he had been at my place often and I did have two rooms. I could use the extra money toward the rent here as well, so I agreed. The rent was still high, but by managing to consolidate down to one premise cost, I would be saving money. I agreed, I did however have him sign a flat mate agreement to share the apartment area.

The detail of the agreement would protect me from and future claims. I wouldn't accuse Martin of entertaining the idea, I just wasn't sure who I could trust. With the lies I had been given by both Kevin and the fundraiser biker group, I had become very sceptical. I had witnessed people's true colours, people whom I would never thought could carry out such havoc. I was still very cut up about the little girl's life. To be honest, I probably needed to talk and seek guidance about some of the goings on I had endured. But I didn't have the time, nor the money, for counselling sessions. Also, the people in my circle of influence seem to have the opinion that you are 'crazy' and 'weak' if you seek counselling.

A customer told me his story once, and I considered it with regard to my own circumstances. He lost half of everything he owned. His girlfriend had moved in with him, eighteen months later and made use of that frivolous relationship time period. She took half of everything he owned. This man was clearly broken. I didn't know what broke him most, the girl leaving him or the fact that she had played him the entire time...I didn't want that to happen, and for some reason, this concept was in the back of my mind.

What harm could come of a flat mate? And a flat mate with an additional perk. He was exceptionally good looking, and occasionally, we would hook up. Also, Kevin had left me alone now that I was spending time with Martin. So, what harm could come about from having him live with me?

The shop was doing well, but needed a financial injection I had to upgrade the toilet area and put in another sink to meet the compliance for a tattoo shop in that area. This meant building another bathroom, as well as a sterilising room. The electrical and plumbing cost the most and had to be certified for the insurances. The modifications proved costly, so I applied for a loan. I set up the new shop, so I could operate and do a lot of the cosmetic building work on the side. I managed to keep the cost down considerably again, only getting in tradesmen when necessary. My daily tasks where abundant and kept me very busy. I would work my standard tattoo day and then work on the modifications over the evening. Cleaning up to be able to trade again the next day. Martin helped me to start with and lost interest after a couple of evenings. He claimed he didn't want to do that type of work all day and come home and have to continue it for my shop.

I could see his point. I also didn't want to encourage the thought or idea that he would be owed or have a say in ownership of the shop. Knowing full well he wanted a joint venture of some sorts... That wasn't going to happen. I already had experienced back handed 'help'. So, I didn't want any help at all. I could do it myself and just plod along. I had no need to hurry and the council had given me ample time to achieve the upgrade.

I didn't set out to neglect any relationships, but was quite happy being consumed by the development of the new tattoo shop. It came together so well and I felt proud about the shop's presentation and vibe. I had done this by myself again. The sense of achievement was so refreshing and I felt like my life was on track once again...

It must have been about five weeks into the new location, when Martin and I had out first difference in opinion. We had considered the idea of extending areas of the tattoo shop into a bar. It was more Martin's concept than mine. I found it easier to listen, rather than closing the idea down. I also felt awkward, as we considered a joined venture between Kevin, Martin and I. Kevin came across as the member that had let down the agreement. So, now Martin considered that we could make a go of a business venture between the two of us... Martin disliked his job and wanted to enter into a business or something of his own. He wanted to place his own efforts and energy into a business, and I understood that. He often pitched negative statements to me about my tattoo shop. I was humbled and very lucky to be able to own my own tattoo shop. And I had worked, and continue to work very hard, on my tattoo shop. I didn't like that approach and anyone who knows me understands that I am a very caring and almost too considerate. This should be a good quality to have, but I disagree. Looking back, I don't believe this is a good attribute to possess at all. It exposes one's vulnerability and it seems that too many people are lined up and waiting to take advantage.

I agreed to be open to the idea but expressed my concerns about drunks in my tattoo shop. I agreed to a progressive plan, hoping that Martin would forget the idea and become consumed in something else within a week or two. Or realise how much effort, time and energy this process would take and be discouraged. Again, I was dancing around actually saying no! I proposed putting just a few beers in a fridge downstairs for a few weeks, to see how everything would pan out. There would have needed to be a huge investment in licensing, not only for the operator of the bar, but for the premise as well. I was not prepared to commit without some thought and exploration of the idea. Anyhow, Martin often came home and had a few cold ales...It was the country's way, beers after work!

This particular evening, Martin had company and was getting quite slurry because of the amount of beer he had consumed. His friends were, also. They were becoming unruly to the extent that I had to draw the line. They came into the tattoo studio area and started behaving like drunk buffoons, whist I was tattooing a customer. The unprofessionalism lead to discounting the job by half price. I had to apologise and had to work to keep the customer after their carry on. That evening, after I cleaned the shop and went to the apartment, I witnessed the first of many disturbing 'Wobblies' thrown by a very drunk Martin. I'm not sure of the exact conversation, but he was not happy that I had asked him to take the 'party elsewhere' in front of his friend. I passed on to him what the evening had cost me financially, and that I didn't see room for a bar or drinking area in my tattoo shop.

Well, I never... I heard the doors slamming, yelling, stomping through rooms and then he went downstairs. He slammed the fridge doors and put my HIFI music system on so loud it nearly took the roof off...I left him to it and had a shower. I was very tired and unimpressed. I too can be hot headed and very stubborn, but I had the forethought to know that the confrontation would lead to chaos. I detested how he was treating my shop. I hadn't finished doing all the modifications to it yet. And he knew how much time I had invested in the upgrade of its presentation. But I left him to his own demise.

I am used to drunk mischief-makers, one of my family members is an exceptional one! The best thing to do is let them sleep it off and pray that they don't work themselves up too much. I had the experience, once, of being woken up, slapped, shaken, yelled in the face, spat on, hugged and then slobbered on, whilst the family member cried, accusing me and the whole world of hating her. All the while, I was coming to from sleeping, so his lordships drunken paddy wasn't really a major issue for me.

The next evening, the silent treatment carried on until he had enough ale under his belt, and he then spat out venomous words about how I had wronged him...I didn't give him credit for how clever he was, he knew what to say to make me question myself. This episode passed but the disorderly behaviour was just unfolding. I banned drinking from the shop during opening hours completely and had to, on many occasions, apologise and discount tattoo work because of the unprofessional behaviour from my so-called boyfriend-flatmate. To spite me, he would come home from work and bring the ale down to the shop, sit there and drink his fill while I was working. I was right to have him sign a housemate agreement. His behaviour was so completely different to what he was like before he moved in. He didn't love or care for me. I actually questioned whether he even liked me as?

This behaviour lasted on and off for 18 months. I had asked him to move on and he would cry and confess his love for me and that he had endured bad things in his past. I don't know why I believed him, but I did.

During the 18 months, I got to know more about his friends. He rode with a few guys and he was very aware of the trials and tribulations I had with the bikers. I had also confided in him the trouble I had with the gangs and that one group kept coming into the shop. Even at the new location, I was visited in my first three weeks. I am against gangs and kept my shop clear of any affiliations. I had signage placed on the entrance, displaying the non-subscription. "No gangs, No patches, No attitudes. Thank you."

I was aware that there was a gang member in Martins family. His ex-wife's side of the family to be exact. He and the mother had a child together, so the family tie or connection was still intact. Martin and the mother had been broken up for over 17 years and I was lead to believe that the relationship thread between him and the family gang member was non-existent; That they rarely rode together or had a beer.

This was seldom and mainly to do with Martin's child. I put two and two together, when I recognised the brother in law. He had come into my shop at the previous location. Before Martin and I had even started talking, before Martin visited me!

Okay, so this is the predicament I was in. I was trying very hard to keep a clean slate and my main focus was on my tattoo shop and its recovery. I was with Martin and I thought it would be easier to let things lie, rather than stand up and confront the situation. And that is how I approached the next few months. The connection was not direct and I had nothing to do with the gang. I talked to my family and was completely honest about my predicament. My dad rode motorcycles, but was an independent rider. He didn't have a need or desire to be connected.

One evening, over a meal, we all talked together about our perspectives. Martin had a good way about him and could verbally stand up for his perspective. His point of view was new to me, and it came to light that he intended to be a part of this biker gang. He had been planning to join them for quite some time. This clashed with every bone in my body. My family seemed to be on board the concept as well, and I felt like I was surrounded by people who I knew so well, but didn't know at all.

I now questioned my values; Was I wrong to be standing up for my own rights? I did not want a gang coming into my shop and demanding my hard earned finances for whatever reason they could justify. Biker gangs treat their women awfully. I remembered what my life was like before I came home. And it was a part of my life I hoped never to re-live again. Did I need to get off my 'crusade' and be okay with these people and their antics? People that use sick children for fundraisers and then pocket the proceeds. They hadn't been the group directly involved with my ordeal, hold on…had they?

Yes it turned out the smaller 'riding group' were actually the 1st point of entry to the larger biker organization…

Martin and I clashed after that conversation. There was a clear divide. He participated and supported the large affiliated biker groups activities... And on weekends, when he used to take off riding, he now advertised to me who he was riding with. He blatantly disrespected me and would ask the patched friends who he rode with to regularly come by my shop and collect him. They would wear their jackets with the labels and insignia and park directly under my sign, "No gangs, No Patches, No Attitudes..." And come into the shop. Some acknowledged me and others wouldn't. I would be working and they would walk straight in to my tattoo shop and home to collect Martin and his bike. Martin had now gained a bottom rocker, which is the under part of the jacket that explains who you are in the bike group. He had placed the insignia on his bike and had no consideration for me or my values. Trying to talk about the topic was the worst thing I could have done. For some reason, the open minded perspective of my family had given Martin the ammunition he needed to completely undermine me and my values.

The day he came in with that bottom 'prospect' rocker on his jacket was the day I formally requested he move out and move on. And, as you can imagine, the request did not run as smoothly as that.

Martin knew my whole story, he had seen how broken I was when I attended the sick little girl's funeral. I couldn't stop crying for days. I was devastated and had to close my tattoo shop. And now I had seen some of the members. They were all familiar faces. They were all present at the fundraiser for the sick little girl. And when I asked him out right if that biker gang was a part of the rider group, he would never answer me straight. He'd tell me to forget it and that I lived in the past too much. He had witnessed it all, he'd seen the treatment I endured from Kevin. He had seen how hard I worked day in and day out. How I strived to provide a professional service and keep out the gangs. Every three months, you could guarantee a member would come into my shop, they wouldn't talk to me, and if they did, they would ask me to tattoo their insignia. I'd stand my ground and refuse politely, every time. I apologised and explained that I was not aligned and merely provided a service to the public.

He knew all this and for him to come home with that bottom rocker was a huge 'middle finger' to me.

This wasn't whimsical and he knew that I felt strongly about biker gangs. We had had lengthy conversations about the expectations, subscriptions, the actions and the consequences of gangs and biker clubs. My perspective of these men in clubs were that they were where men who were too weak to stand alone in life. They carried out immoral tasks and joined together for strength in numbers. Their treatment of women was repulsive and their self-promoted societal hierarchy was absurd. I still feel this way today, and if any one of those men were placed into a predicament where the 'killing field' was even, I am sure you would witness a very different outcome.

One time, Martin and I had gone for some lunch at the city's harbour. When we arrived, I discovered the bikers that Martin had contacts with were at one of the restaurant-bars. There were around 20 men in leather, all advertising who they were. I was surprised to see this was allowed in the classy area of the city. Martin was called over straight away, he looked at me and told me to go with him and have a drink. I said I wouldn't and would wait by the water's edge for him. I had a tiny reputation, but our city is small, so hearsay and gossip travels. That third degree of separation reference can be applied to our small country. You can guarantee that someone will know someone who knows you. I am quite colourful, I visually stand out and am easily recognised. I didn't want to be seen with this group at all. At this stage, I was privy to the extent of the tantrums that Martin could throw and although he was unimpressed with me, we were in the middle of the city and he couldn't possibly be seen to be treating his girlfriend badly in public. I stood by myself near the railing by the water, while he had a beer, took his time and ordered another. He starred at me, whilst he drank and laughed. This unspoken action was for me to understand 'my place' and for me to join him, no argument. I did one better than that. I went to the car and left him there. I jingled the keys as I walked past, again to gesture I was leaving. He did and said nothing to me. Some of the members that he was with him shouted insults at me and called me a dog as I walked by. I knew from that point I had made yet another huge mistake. There was no love for me from him at all. Which brought me to this question: So why was he with me?

I had typed a letter and handed it to him, when he arrived back later that day. I had packed my car and organised to stay with a friend for a couple of days. I was sure this would be the action that broke the camel's back. The paddy this time could possibly be hospitalising for me. After handing him the letter, I raced to the car and drove up the drive, as fast as I could.

My heart was pounding, I couldn't believe I had done it. I went to my girlfriend's and had a stiff whiskey. The text messages started flying to my phone. Twenty three in total for that night, all threatening, not a nice word in any of them... How on earth can one human treat another like this? Isn't he meant to love me? Is this love? Did I bring this on myself? Why am going around in circles...My choices are so bad, what's wrong with me, what am I missing?

He promised in his text messages to trash my apartment and level my tattoo shop. I guess he kept his promise. I planned to go and stay away from home for a couple of days, hoping to avoid the next part of the ordeal. But I decided to go the next morning. I figured it would be best to go and face him the next day rather than put it off. I was living on nervous energy and if I dealt with it all today, hopefully it wouldn't overflow into my working week. Fingers crossed.

Every door was kicked in and dented in the apartment, holes from thrown fists in the walls, shelving and ornaments broken. I was there 5 minutes, and as I came out of my room, the hot water kettle was heaved at my head. It kind of jerked out of the wall, which made jug veer off and miss me. Lucky for me. Unsatisfied with that, he came at me to assault me with a closed fist. I had backed into the bedroom doorway. I stood there motionless, looking at him. I didn't flinch or cry,

I just stood there. I was prepared to take a beating. I just stood there looking at him ready to collect the blow.

He stopped himself. Right then and there something happened, I didn't cower or flinch, I was ready to take another thrashing from a man with doubled my own strength and I wasn't timid!

I went to walk passed him, I had to, there was no other way out of the apartment. He started to cry, which was also a regular emotion; First the paddy then the anger, the rage and then the cry, then the sex, a little sleep and feeding time again... He was just a big baby. What a bloody child! He bear hugged me, confessing his love and how sorry he was...

I had asked him officially to move out and end the relationship. He had said NO. It would seem that his NO meant NO and my no, meant nothing...

In my mind, I was weighing up whether I just lay there and take it again or fight. I was worried about his rage and was sure if I resisted the ordeal would get worse. Anyway, is it not a woman's prerogative to lay there and take it, whatever a man wants a man gets? I didn't know any different. Is it not part and parcel of being a woman? Doing what the man wants? I used to enjoy being intimate with my partner, but that was drummed out of in my mid-twenties. I tend to just do what I think is expected of me nowadays. I can honestly say, that I have never had a loyal considerate man who really cared for me, ever!

Shop Shot'

12

Silly me, I'd been set up from the beginning

It took me seven weeks to get Martin out of my apartment, from the day I issued him with the appeal on paper. I had to come up with an astute plan, as he blatantly refused my demand.

We sought counselling, as he said he wanted to get some help. We booked a counselling session and attended. As soon as I mentioned the gang affiliation, the counsellor wrapped up our meeting and referred me to the assisted income city counselling service. The counsellor informed us that she was not prepared to take on any case of this content...I made another appointment with the city counselling service and we both attended. I was not sure what to expect and was disappointed in the pass-the-parcel result from our first counselling session. At the assisted income city counselling service, our assigned councillor lady had run over our expected meeting time by half an hour, this made us both late for our jobs, as we had to meet their schedule times and not ours. The service was only available during the standard week days' work hours, which made meeting times hard to arrange.

Our counsellor did almost all of the talking during our first session, educating us to repeating cycles and effective communication. Instead of using defensive and objectifying communication, that would create a negative agenda, when we exchange dialogue with each other. We were also asked to engage in communication activities. This was similar to trust building games I played in school. We were to tell each other the concerns we had and look at how we were responding to the way the concern was delivered. This was not what I had in mind at all. I wanted to get to the root of the problem, the subscription to the gang and why I had been manipulated into a situation that I did not want in my life; No dancing around the outskirts of the problem with conversation deliverables and outcomes. The problem was that one person in this relationship had a want and aspiration, and the other had opposing desire. Not only had that, one party considered themselves far more superior than the other, therefore, not entertaining what the other person was requesting! Martin had knowingly tricked me into a predicament, rather than being up front and honest. I didn't want to continue this relationship and that was what we should have been discussing.

We left the unsuccessful counselling session and both went back to our jobs. I was trying to avoid spending time with Martin and often spent the evening with friends at their houses. I'd stay the night and go to work when my customers were due to arrive. My poor tattoo shop was at the bottom of the priority list again. It was a means to earning a living and accessing my goals and aspirations. Yet, they had been pushed aside yet again. I had let my personal life leak all over my professional life...

I would get up and go the other room, when Martin came to sleep beside me. I was trying to let him know that I didn't want anything to do with him anymore. That our relationship had ended. He pretended nothing was wrong. And I was completely baffled as to why he wouldn't accept it and move on? WHY?

We had to do six sessions with the counsellor. That was mandatory and part of the program for abusive situations and dysfunctional families. There was a subsidy granted with the cost providing and we were expected to participate in all six counselling sessions. I didn't mind that at all. I just expected that we would get down to some key life factors that had collapsed our world. I wanted to own what I had done wrong and find out how to fix things. I didn't want to live this turbulent lifestyle that I had. I wished for a more peaceful environment. Therefore, I welcomed the counselling sessions.

Having been disappointed with our last session, I called the counsellor and asked if I could have a meeting without Martin. She agreed and we scheduled it in. I wanted to communicate with her the point where I considered us to be at in the relationship. I asked if the sessions could be tailored more toward us both going our own separate ways, rather than trying to rectify the communication between us. I also needed her to understand the paddies that he threw, or fits of rage. I was very concerned, as these were even worse when he drank. And at the moment, with the relationship at an end, he was drinking quite a lot. I also suspected that Martin was not in a relationship with me because he had been attracted to me as a person. I felt that there was an agenda there, and that it had something to do with the biker gang he was now prospecting for.

In this counselling session, I was going to make sure that I was the one who would do the talking and educate the counsellor to what was the circumstances were. I wanted to be heard and understood. I wanted this man out of my apartment and away from me. He had said NO outright to my demand. He was not leaving!

The counsellor was late again that day for my appointment. This was exactly what I needed to express disappointment. I was so stunned by the lack of professionalism and was ready to express what I expected from their counselling services. I questioned whether her blatant disregard for poor time keeping was due to who I was? That I was a tattoo artist, who had a partner, who was now a member of a gang and maybe I wasn't good enough for her to keep her appoint time? Although I have many tattoos, I have good presentation, dress well and am punctual.

I requested that the councillor lady listen to what I had to say and take action or advise accordingly.

This took her by surprise, as I addressed the areas in front of her reception staff, in a very polite but direct manner. I told her of some of the goings on in our relationship. I told her it was all a sham, he didn't love me and I was on the way to losing my shop. This was the truth. I may be slow, but I am not stupid. That gang had been trying to get into my tattoo shop for years. Tattoo shops pay area royalties and protection money. And that is why he wouldn't leave.

I provided a copy of the request to move out. I had also prepared a signed letter of exactly what I wanted to achieve with the counselling sessions. I included photographs of abuse, damage and a patched member outside my shop and under my sign. I also provided the initial flat-share agreement stating, that although he was living with me as my boyfriend, the housemate agreement would supersede any periodic or relationship connection that would entitle him to possessions that I may own. And he had signed it and dated it. I also explained about the experience of the 'hit' on my shop, the little girl and the biker group that kept the raised money. And that the people were all linked together. Martin was Kevin's so- called friend and was linked to both the riding club and the biker gang. I had heard through the grape vine, that the riding group was a primary bike group to-do with an initiation process for the biker gang. I also informed the councillor that the police were keeping a close eye on me since the 'hit' ordeal and that maybe that was why nothing worse had happened to me.

The letter detailed the removal of Martin from my home, my business and my life. We had been advised to do the six week programme, before making any decisions. I was adamant that I wanted this relationship terminated. I had a signed a dated letter addressed to the assisted income city counsellor. I informed the counsellor that Martin would attend next week's meeting as arranged, but I would not be attending; That Martin was to be informed that he was not to return to the apartment after that meeting. He could have the week to arrange someone to pick up his belongings on his behalf. He had very little, so this was not a big task. I gave them $3000.00 dollars for him. This was to cover his bond and so he had the finances to be able to find accommodation immediately. After that meeting, I would continue attending the remaining counselling sessions on my own. My councillor was never late again.

The morning of the counselling session that I knew I was not attending, I was very panicky. I prayed that the system would aid me in removing this man out of my life. I was losing everything, I couldn't manage staff, my work load and the repairs to the tattoo shop, let alone the inner turmoil I carried. *"My suitcase of personal baggage harboured so much negativity it was bursting at the seams...How did I let me life get so out of hand?"* I was on the brink of failing my tattoo shop. Martin had a different agenda, and I didn't give him credit for how cunning he could be. I thought I had carefully planned a way out aided by the counselling system. He was also using the counselling system to implicate and set me up. He was going for the 'take over' of my tattoo shop.

In this country, you need two signatures from close relatives or next of kin to be placed into psychiatric care. Martin had carefully assembled the necessary paperwork to apply to have me taken into care. All he needed was my father's signature. The day of the planned counselling session that I had no intention of attending. I was caught completely off guard. My father had called me to inform me that Martin had arrived at his place of work. Martin was claiming that I had gone 'crazy', and that he needed my father's signature to get me some help. I really needed help and he had organised everything for me. Although I kept most information from my family as I didn't want to concern them, I did make them aware of my plan to enforce Martin's departure from my life. I had also well-informed my dad that there wasn't any other way. I had been to see the police and explored every avenue to remove this person from my life. The counselling steps were a system that was part of a process for women, children and families in my predicament, or worse. At this point, I was very glad that I hadn't kept my plans details hidden from my father. Martin was partitioning to have me placed in psychiatric care and all he needed was one family member's signature and his own.

My dad wasn't aware that he had been served a formal notice by the counsellor not to return to my address, nor that I had given him the finances to be able to find a new home straight away. And Martin did not offer that information to him either.

Again, my issues were spilling out onto others. My Dad had been perturbed at his work again...At this stage, with all that had gone on, I was open to the diagnosis of being labelled 'crazy'. Take me away and lock me up; I was over living this nightmare.

Martin was very smart. He had befriended my friends and family, and had been planning all along to coax me to let him have participation in my business. My friends would confront me with stories that had been fabricated. As I had little time for any of this, I withdrew from them. I considered them to be prying acquaintances, rather than friends. And to my amazement, I was surrounded by them all, wanting to put in their own personal two cents worth of opinions about what was supposedly happening in my life. Martin had used the couple of personal days I had taken to mourn the sick little girl who lost her battle to leukaemia. And emphasised how upset I was, to paint a picture that I was constantly upset and hysterical. Martin had an agenda from the start.

Anyone who has ever ran or managed a service providing business, would know that you do not have any time to be sick, upset or mournful, as this conduct has a direct reflection on the business productivity. I strived every day to ensure all my customers received the best service, and that my team maintained the most professional atmosphere that I could possibly provide. I sheltered them from the turbulence, and tried to manage any obstacle that arose.

The counselling efforts were not the end of the turbulence, as I had hoped. Eventually, the police stepped in and Martin was forced from my life. Not without getting in a good couple of incidents first, he had to make sure he left me broken...And that he did!

Weekly, I had to earn $1000.00 dollars to meet the overheads. Rain, hail or shine, this had to be met, but the commotions of my life were taking their toll. I sought contentment in the small areas, like the presentation of my tattoo shop. I had some fixing up to do, but that didn't take me too long to get organised. I had dissociated from my friends and found that most of them were too opinionated with no real understanding of the situation. Their opinions were based more on Martin's version of events. He was travelling around, visiting them and regaling his side of the story and painting me as idiotic. To top it off, Kevin had also done the same and still kept in contact with a couple of people that were my so-called long term friends...

When I did, eventually, catch up with some friends, of course they told me who was saying what. I think they relished the drama of it all, to be honest. It came to light that Martin and Kevin were friends the whole time, and I started piecing together the puzzle. I was very aware that Martin wanted my tattoo shop. He had tried every angle to get part ownership of it. He even tried to get his family members involved as contractors and potential clients. I had tried to be smart and keep my shop apart from the relationship, but was unsuccessful.

I had been set up from the start, the biker gang wanted my shop and to use my credentials. If they had been successful, my tattoo shop would have become another gang owned tattoo shop! They would have moved in, taken a large portions of the earnings and, more than likely, pilot their illegal businesses using my tattoo shop as a frontage...I had been set up from the very beginning!

13
My circle of influence, maybe not the most conducive surroundings

I always considered a relationship to be give and take. No matter what relationship it may be: partner, friend, co-worker or other. Participants need to invest a certain amount of effort to ensure that a relationship remains formidable. Most of my friend relationships felt one sided. I was visited when someone wanted something, not because they wanted to see me.

I thought, perhaps, I was the conundrum. I am happy to acknowledge any problem I may cause and am willing to find out how to remedy that problem. I am very open to change and to trying to make positive transformations.

I had many visitors, but not the friends who I had hoped would visit me. I figured maybe my life's commotion made people feel uneasy, and they didn't really want to be subjected to any of it, which was fair enough too. I do admit I had changed since the death of my mother and the opening of my tattoo shop. I found myself overwhelmed with all of the 'goings' on'.

I seldom drank and going out to get intoxicated each weekend had lost its value. This way of life also seemed almost pathetic to me. Which meant I had grown apart from the circle of friends that were in my life. Some felt that I came across as too good and thought myself better than them. This was never true, I was only concerned with doing what was 'right'. I had taken on a big responsibility with owning and running a tattoo shop. I also had other people who relied on me to manage my tattoo shop effectively, and I wanted to the best job possible. And if that meant making hard decisions and changing my way of life to suit owning and maintaining a business, then I would oblige.

I really can't understand why people need conformity amongst their social groups.

I personally find variances, opinions and observations interesting. I don't want to feel that I should endorse their extracurricular undertakings and recreational habits.

I personally chose to live a different life. I didn't judge or have anticipations of them to become like me; so why did they expect me to conform to their way of life? And why did I have to condone their 'illegal' activities in my life or around my business? They are supposed to be my friends!

Not one of these people had worked hard towards anything, what they had in their life had been given to them. And by that time, I had enough of all of it, and I was ready to make a big change. Too much damage had been done.

My business' name was again stained, but this time, by the local drop kicks and hangers on, who claimed to be my friends. I was judged and despised for not wanting them linked to me, or my tattoo shop. I'd like to encourage some thought here; about why we have expectations of other people. Especially our friends, when we do not clearly communicate our said expectation. We assume 'that is' the way things are. And we assume that the other person or party has subscribed to our way. In turn, we are then offended when it is not so…

We do not communicate and check whether the understanding of our expectation has been accepted or subscribed to. And why do we expect everyone to conform to our way?

I didn't have anyone in my circle of influence that I could converse with on a mature level. And this led to a divide between me and a lot of my friends. Most of them still went out, smoked a lot of weed and indulged in other recreational activities. I had changed, as I had gained something in my life that I did not want to lose. And wreckless activities could have resulted in my business negligence. I did not want to take that gamble and opted for change.

I had received a great deal of backlash, ridicule and unpleasantness from these people, who called themselves my friends for many years. I had expected that to a degree. And I thanked them for their actions, that had helped me to see clearly who they are.

Although their actions injured me, I have had time to heal and I would not change a single occurrence.

This wasn't an easy process to undertake. I was scared and thought I would be lonely forever. I considered that I would feel a huge void in my life. And that the negative banter would have an effect on my tattoo shop for sure.

But I was surprised. It did not and I did not feel that lonely. Instead, I felt free of demands, with no pressure and a sense of release.

I made simple changes and started making different choices. For example, the colours of clothing that I would wear and genres of music that I wanted to like, I gave them a go. My exchanges at work were lighter and easy. I was happy to spend time chit chatting to customers and enjoying my career. I had more time to spend on my design work. I concluded in my mind, that if this was 'lonely' then I liked it! My cell phone list was shorter and my social media friends fewer, but other than that, the loss of friends had no real impact on my happiness. In fact, their departure increased my happiness and this was a very nice surprise!

I focused solely on my tattoo shop. I knew I had to identify what I wanted in my life and cut away everything else. And that is what I did. I focused on small and enjoyable tasks like a favourite song in the morning, the type or brand of coffee I liked, the TV shows I preferred. I pleased myself, rather than anyone else. I didn't consider anyone. And if a matter arose that wasn't to do with my tattoo shop or my family, then I didn't entertain it.

I made lists of what I wanted. Lists of what to consider when confronted with a decision. What my focus was and current circumstances are. The questions I should be asking when seeking advice, and whether the person I sought advice from may be qualified to give the perspective or advice. Or could it be possible that they may have an agenda of their own? Also, I took a look at my circle of concern and who was influential in my life...Who they were, what they had in their lives, what had they achieved...and if they were worthy of my time. It was time to value myself.

I wanted to be the strong, enthusiastic and the internally beautiful person I used to be. Not this insecure, untrusting, lifeless, numb carcass I had become. I figured I would be honest and let people know that I wasn't sure who I could trust. And I was now taking the time I needed...I would leave the choices up to the other people, and if they wanted to be in my life, then great. But I had no interest in subscribing to anything they expected of me. This meant, they would have to be patient and respectfully give me the time I required to develop a relationship with them. Those who had a problem, or had demands of me, could be forgotten about. I have an aversion to admitting this material, but ninety percent of my so-called friends fell into that category. My lifetime would not become desirable, if my circle of influence did not change. I would not grow or achieve my intended goals, if I did not actively make a change.

And it seemed that no-one in my circle of influence wanted me to take the time to organise my life. They turned out to be a nasty bunch of people. I am very happy to have come to that realisation, although the process was agonising.

Even now, I have no interest in having large quantities of friends. I am happy and appreciative of the few people in my life.

"The positive affirmations on social media and large friend numbers are a nice attribute to have.

But don't deserve to be given any weight. They are what they are.

Just numbers and likes..." – Jaimie Diamond

14
Here we go again

I find the older I get, the more I realise I know absolutely nothing at all...The calming period was short-lived and the turbulence tap had been turned on yet again.

I had more visits from gangs, especially one in particular. Yes, the biker gang that Martin was connected with. My car window was smashed again, I was abused verbally in my tattoo shop and ordered to close and leave town. I was also instructed that I was not to provide the tattoo service anymore from my tattoo shop. The car containing the instructive occupants drove their maroon people-moving van down the driveway, and blocked my tattoo shop entrance door. They came into my tattoo shop and verbally provided me with their very clear expectations.

Additionally, a week or so later, I had an older couple, that were friends of my mother, call in for a coffee. They knew of my tattoo shop and that I aimed to provide a professional service. They themselves were not into tattoo art, but understood the popularity of tattoos as some of their children had acquired a couple. They had helped me with electrical advice during my tattoo shop upgrade and it was lovely to see them again. I was honoured that they felt comfortable enough to stop by the tattoo shop to have a coffee.

Whilst we were all having coffee and a chat, I had some unexpected visitors come in. *"Talk about timing".*

Two gang members come into the shop 5 minutes after my mother's friends had come in. *"No, not now, please. Not now"* I thought.

Straight away, the shop felt uneasy. I said hello and asked the two members to let me know if I could help them with anything. They looked around my tattoo shop and enquired about insignia tattoo work. I politely apologised and declined the service or that type of tattoo work. One of the men was very tall, he looked like he could have been a kick boxer. Slender, toned and very strong. He came back at me in an argumentative manner. Telling me it was my job to do tattoos and he wanted to get a tattoo. I explained that the tattoo shop was my own and that I provided artwork tailored to the customer. That the artwork I provided did not include gang affiliated lettering, symbols or logos. And I had the right to decline any work, if I did not feel comfortable doing it.

My heart was pounding by this stage, my mouth had become dry and the words were hard to form, let alone deliver *"Please leave, please leave"* I was praying..."*Not now, don't do anything now in front of my mum's friends, please*".

I also managed to say in stern but polite manner. Once you have had a look around, I would like you to leave, please. I looked the bigger guy straight in the eye when I said this. I was half expecting him to head butt me, or hook punch me in the mouth. He gave me a hard stare and then they left. My mother's friends commended me on the management of the situation, little did they know it was a regular occurrence. And that I may have just provoked the biker gang even more. They left shortly after, and I apologised profusely for their encounter. I was sure that they would not return for a coffee again. "They never did!"

A few weeks after that incident, another couple came in from the same gang. I was expecting another visit, so this was not a surprise. I had asked them to leave in an assertive manner. This would have been seen as a dictation and would not have been digested favourably...

The gang member that came in this time was a large, ethnic, beefy man with long untamed hair, really long hair, in a messy plait that came down past the bottom of his leather jacket. He had a skinny girl along with him. She trailed behind him in bare feet and barely dressed. She looked muddy, unwashed and carried the signs of heavy drug use. He looked around my tattoo shop. Again, I said, "Hello" and greeted him. I try to greet everyone who comes into the tattoo shop. I am a big believer of first impressions. A warm smile and nice welcome works wonders. And I don't limit my greetings, everyone gets one!

As the man walked the circumference of the tattoo shop, he did not make eye contact or acknowledge that I had spoken to him. He grabbed at the girl, who was fixated on one wall's tattoo design. She kept pointing at it. He grabbed her throat, demonstrating his authority, and she was slapped around the head like a naughty child. The girl fidgeted around so much, she was clearly off of her head on drugs or something. He walked out and whistled to her. As you would calling a dog. When he got to the entrance dorm he shouted "come – female dog!" This was purely a demonstration and message for me. The message was that I am nothing more than a dog to them. Maybe that I should obey?

I had many unpleasant encounters, and looking back now, I do not know how I repeatedly picked myself up and carried on with life. Another event was when I had the biker gang stand in front of my trade stand at a big tattoo convention. They blocked my trade site, stopping me from gaining any walk–in customers. Generally, at trade shows, I have my customers pre-booked. This gives the notion that I am a very busy shop, however, this year, I decided to be a little bit different. I had noticed that there was a lot of general public who enquired about getting tattoos performed at the tattoo convention, and not many shops supplied the walk-in demand. So, this year, I had geared up to supply walk-in tattoos at the show. *"How cool is that, getting a little tattoo at the convention, I would like to get one as well and maybe add the date too… Awesome!"*

I had a tattoo walk-in's welcome sign made for my trade stand.

And three big patched thugs stood at the entrance of my allocated trade stand with their arms crossed, giving me the evil eye. I had paid $1200.00 dollars for the trade site alone and was hoping to restore a little positivity back toward my tattoo shop. The burly blokes wearing their patches stood there intentionally to intimidate me.

It worked. I was worried for my sign written car in the car park, my trade site and equipment. That my team had to endure this unwelcome behaviour and what this must have looked like to other people at the show. My potential customers...

I couldn't cope anymore. I went to the bathroom, having a panic attack and then throwing up. I couldn't afford anymore strife from these people. My insurance premiums were through the roof from the claims I had made replacing the damage done to my car and tattoo shop. My team were becoming unsettled and questioning my management and their safety. My customers were also dropping like flies, as they did not want to endure any part of what they may be subjected to. And the rumours were railing around, growing and morphing for a more dramatic story.

"Breathe, Jaimie, you have to get back out there. You can't leave your team on their own". Get back out there is what I did.

My resident thugs accompanied my trade site for an hour or so. From the time the tattoo show opened to a little bit after lunch. I told the security staff of the convention and the bikers were advised to move on. They walked past, eyeballing me for the remainder of the day. Martin had joined them by that afternoon. I was shaking on the inside, but tried not to show any emotion. I just focused on the customers I was working on and tried to provide a great experience, as well as lead by example for my team. The tattoo shows, that I adored so much, had also become tarnished by the biker gang bullying antics. This is so wrong on every level. *"I pray to any 'god' for a change"!*

Shop Shot'

15

It's not worth the fight, I'm closing my tattoo shop

Toward the end of my 6th year in business, and having endured such a tempestuous time with owning the tattoo shop, I had come to a point where I had to make some major life-altering decisions. And not just change my circle of friends. I had focused so much on the running of my tattoo shop. That my own artistic growth 'goal' had been shelved permanently. My intentions were there, however, I could never seem to juggle all the balls to achieve the goals I wanted.

There were constant overheads, not forgetting the interest accumulating debt that was growing at an unstoppable rate. And as soon as I got back on track, some incident would happen.

I was so very tired and couldn't take any time off.

As soon as I stopped working, the income stopped as well. I hadn't managed to maintain a productive team of tattoo artists either.

I needed contract tattoo artists, who were able to work autonomously. My lead by example approach meant that I worked hard and they watched me…In fact, I think I inherited children with the amount of hand holding I had to do with my contracting tattoo artists. I think they saw what was going on and took advantage of the situation.

Maybe I had the wrong team. I was not selective enough in my choice and I was too soft.

I believe in the sincerity of people's words and have the compassion that everyone makes mistakes. Maybe I didn't spend enough time with them? I found that I couldn't stamp out their negative mentality, even in my own tattoo shop. And I grew very tired with the constant combat with artist attitudes. I attracted the incompetent, insecure artists, who wanted to prioritise gossip and recreational drug use over providing a good tattoo service.

I hoped to attract beautiful artists, that wanted a comfortable working environment. A well-managed shop, where they could create and produce tattoo master pieces; Inspire a team that could grow together and become a renowned team of highly skilled artists...That was my aim.

I had tailored the remunerations for the artists benefit with contributions to the overheads, rather than a specific profit percentage. Eager to create an artistic family, rather than making money off of my contractor artists.

I had my own clientele and worked equally as hard as they did. I had the purest of intentions. But my high expectations were maybe too high? I'm sad to admit that I was unsuccessful. I never attracted any artist with the aspiration, commitment or willingness to put in the effort necessary to become a really good tattoo artist. Constantly managing the team hindered my progression to that goal, also.

I was taking two steps back and only one forward. I really wanted to have a professional tattoo shop, where I could push and explore my artistic capacity. Yet, my time management didn't give me the luxury to develop new skills, explore new equipment or styles that were developing in the tattoo world. I didn't have the time to personally advance my skills and that was the main aim of owning my own tattoo shop.

To top things off, the tattoo industry popularity saw an influx of budding new artists. Some of which were phenomenally talented! I mean outstanding, artistically gifted artists. I knew I had to step up my level of tattoo service but never managed to make the time to invest in myself.

Also, new tattooists were setting up and providing the tattoo services from home. These home working tattooists are classed as backyard-tattooists. They were darting up everywhere. The home tattoo services was under cutting the shop prices by a hefty margin. They weren't providing the best quality in tattoo productivity but many people didn't seem to care.

There was a new rivalry that had developed in the tattoo industry.

The legitimate tattoo shops vs the backyard-tattooists. And as there were are relaxed regulations in our country, there was nothing in place to stop backyard operators. So, the rivalry took precedent.

I am on the side of the tattoo shop, not only because I own one and poured my heart and soul into my tattoo shop, but also because of the concerns around the health and safety. The cross-contamination aspect of the tattoo industry is very important. We deal with blood pathogens and cross contaminations similar to a dentist or doctor's surgery. I had registered my business and obtained a health license. I had to execute areas and processes for compliance. So, setting up from a home environment with relaxed and inadequate sterilising processes in place is not only a possible hazard to the customer, but a huge risk to the family occupying the home also...

Considering every circumstance, I came to my conclusion. As an artist, I had become stagnant and I did not want my life's content to be made up of this constant battle.

I wanted my effort and energy put into my artwork and my personal artistic developments.

It dawned on me, why was I still fighting for my shop? It didn't give me what I desired. So, what was the point of fighting? For a name? So I can beat my chest and say I own a tattoo shop? Give me a break! I couldn't care less about the status or ownership.

I cared about the service and the artwork. I didn't need to own a tattoo shop for that, so WHY was I keeping it open?

And with that thought, I made up my mind to close. I could have sold my tattoo shop, but it would break my heart to see it taken over by a local bunch of gang members. And I didn't think my heart could take to much more anguish. I had hit the point of needing some reparation time. I hoped to experience some of the good in life and feel inspired again.

I decided to close my tattoo shop two months shy of being open for 7 years.

As soon as I had made the decision, I was astounded at how relieved I felt.

Closing the shop was a process in itself. I had to close and finalise accounts. Advertise to finish people's artwork and honour or refund any business gift vouchers the shop had sold. The whole process took around 6 months. I planned to sell up and attempt to clear as much of my accumulated debt as possible.

I had lined up work in the next country. One of the towns had a busy shop and had just opened another branch. I applied for the position and was given the job instantly. And to my delight, they were independently owned. With no biker gang problems.

Closing the shop was tough and costly, as the day to day overheads were still there and had to be met. Sadly, when you close a business and try to do it the correct way without claiming bankruptcy, or just walking away from your financial obligations. It is very difficult. News spreads fast and customers are not that sympathetic. I was clutching at monetary straws and welcomed any work or help.

I had an artist approach me, who had just come back from overseas. He was well known and I had known him for around 10 years.

He had been in the tattoo industry a lot longer than I had been and generally had my respect. He saw where I was at with the business, and wanted to rent a part of the shop for some of his clientele. So, I considered renting space out to him in my last few months. It would be cheaper to rent part of my shop to him, than him setting up his own.

He too felt spent and disheartened with the tattoo industry and had his own industry demons. Now he was back in his home country, he wanted to ease back into work.

He claimed to have lots of work from the town's naval base, and I believed the sincerity of his words. Another mistake on my behalf.

Of course he didn't have two dimes to rub together, so the talk of opening a shop was a complete load of lies. I let him use my shop and stay in the upstairs apartment. A 'two for one' deal. He could work and live over the next few months, costing him $200 dollars per week toward my overheads. This was for both the accommodation and the use of the tattoo shop, power, utilities and internet access. Cheap I know, but hey, I intended to close and figured 'pay it forward' and it will come back, right...wrong! "So very wrong"!

I was wrapping up the shop and traveling around the country to arranged destinations, finishing off any unfinished tattoo work that I had started. I hired space at other shops to make sure I did my best at tying up any of my tattoo artwork loose ends. I wanted to do right by my business, more so for my customers. I was away for eight weeks, and when I returned, I intended to hand over the shop premise to the real estate agent. I would move the furniture out to sell, hopefully recouping some money back.

Before I returned, the fellow tattoo artist, the friend I had living and working from my tattoo shop, sent me a message via SMS.

The friend claimed he had no money and the shop had no customers coming in...He intended to leave before I arrived back... And you guessed it, he didn't pay a cent of any money he owed. The last and final pain he caused me was the huge power bill he had accumulated and my furniture that he took with him. *"The... little Bleep!"*

This confirmed it. I had made the right choice.

I closed up the shop and welcomed a new beginning.

16
A little bit of insight as a female tattoo artist

Going back to when I selected my career as a tattoo artist, I admit, as a young girl, I was fascinated by the gang and biker lifestyle. I found myself magnetised to the bad boy image. The big bikes and their force of nature presence had a certain appeal to it. I seemed to be surrounded by this genre of people during my tattoo apprenticeship, so it was natural to be intrigued by this lifestyle.

As I grew into an individual, independent and confident lady, I struggled with the blatant obvious degradation of women.

There is a clear divide amongst these type of men and women. It wouldn't matter if you were their wife, daughter, sister or mother, you are considered to be less significant than the fellow male bikers. The TV show, 'Sons of Anarchy,' provides a great visual perspective of this.

Women, in general, are perceived to be on a lower stratum in comparison to men, especially when working in tattoo shops. I knew this from the get-go and quickly understood my place in life in the tattoo world as a female.

Both my parents worked and I was taught to believe that I should consider myself as an equal. Women working and having independence was growing more common. So, the mindset that encouraged me to consider myself on a lower level than some of my acquaintances was hard for me to accept.

Especially, when some of the people I was surrounded were more Neanderthal than man.

I have always had a clear understanding of right and wrong. As a youngster, I knew how to treat others and have always tried to treat other people how I would like to be treated in return. Again, a lead by example approach if ever presented with uncertainty. Having been headstrong from a young age, and now working in the environment that I was, the education to the alternative, hierarchal way, was different. What one should tolerate and what was to be acceptable conflicted me. I always wanted to be a tattoo artist, but it seemed that the career I had chosen had an underlying expectation for me to conform to a lifestyle that I did not support. This was not abundantly clear in the beginning, however.

All of a sudden, I was confronted with this competitive fight. And I was in a game, where I couldn't back down. This fight was for customers, jobs and status. This fight determined how much or how little you earned. This fight determined whether you made it in the tattoo industry.

I had just come out of my tattoo apprenticeship, so I was on the bottom of the food chain, so to speak. But I hadn't had the time to fine tune any particular tattoo genre or style as a tattoo artist. I had no point of difference. This meant I would only be 'fed' the small tattoos in the shop that no-one wanted to do. And only on the proviso that the other artists had enough work, otherwise, I wouldn't be given any work at all!

I decided to use my initiative. I was working on a couple of tattoos, where the customers let me tattoo them with my own designs, that allowed me to further my skill by doing their tattoo at a discounted price. I would forfeit my percentage and still pay the shop theirs. This allowed me to take on a few larger tattoo pieces and implement my own tattoo style. I would design artwork known as flash art and advertise my own tattoo art designs.

I made sure that I didn't draw anything too elaborate. I had already encountered hierarchy amongst my co-workers. And the biggest slap in the face was when I personally designed tattoo art pieces and they were given to another artist to perform because, apparently, I was not up to that level of tattoo yet. The worst part was, I was naive and let this happen. I thought that was normal during an apprenticeship. The tattoo artist didn't even give me $50 dollars for the design, yet he earned $800 plus dollars from it. So, a little note to anyone who is undertaking a tattoo apprenticeship: This is not normal, you do not have to give over your designs to artists who have been working longer than you. If you are not at a stage where you are able to perform your tattoo design, then wait until you are, or sell it to the artist. I wish I had stood up for myself a little sooner.

You learn to be thick skinned as a tattoo artist and, eventually, the time comes when you will stand up for you self. I have met many artists and lots with magnanimous egos; mostly males, but some females too.

If you have any potential as an artists, you will encounter negative commentaries. I received plenty toward me and my tattoo work. I personally welcome feedback, and took the opinion that one can only grow. If I am not educated to areas that need attention or growth, then how can I expand my skills, right? I am open to new techniques and ideas and I welcome the education from any friend or foe. Unfortunately, the delivery from some fellow artists cupped with a heavy dose of ego can be an awful experience. I have had many tattoo 'gods' or artists, that I have held in high stead for years, crumble and shatter my opinion of them.

They have now become nothing more than filth in my eyes; Scum who shouldn't have the gift to be a tattoo artist. Sadly, if you have even the tiniest amount of potential as a tattoo artist, you will encounter the older generation of tattoo artists, that may want to cut you down and will probably try to hinder you more so than help you.

I have been challenged in front of my customers and fellow contracting artists to draw without using tracing paper, claiming that I cannot draw. That I only trace and shouldn't be a tattooist...As instructed, to prove myself as an artist, I welcomed the challenge to draw with no aid. The pessimistic fellow artist giving the order possibly needed some improvement in this area himself and the negative focus came full circle. He ended up looking very silly. As I sat there and drew a fantasy art dragon from scratch right in front of everyone with no tracing paper, no reference or light box.

Some artist mentors have shown me inaccurate ways to perform tattoos, made me tattoo almost impossible areas of the body when I was inexperienced, or perform a tattoo with a brand of machine I was not used to. I had been misinformed on machine tuning. Some shops will try to dictate what style of tattoo machine you use.

If you apprentice in a shop that uses a main type of machine for example coils only, then it is likely as an apprentice that you will pick up that type of machine also. So, if you later join another tattoo shop and are instructed to use a different type of tattoo machine, such as a swash, this can be very foreign to you. The goal here is generally intending to keep your skill levels of tattooing from advancing. You can learn and probably will learn to use many types of tattoo machines in your time as a tattoo artist. Providing you stick with becoming a tattoo artist. *"And that is the hard part"*.

I came to the understanding that this was an unspoken rule, you never help any other artist. What if they become good or better than you?

I have always had more concern for the customer. Where is the consideration for the customer, who is receiving the tattoos, and why isn't the main focus on understanding and providing exactly what he or she wants? The people that are paying us to execute their tattoo.

Admittedly, when I learned to tattoo, there was an older generation and style of tattooing. Tattooing and the equipment has advanced considerably today. The new generation of tattoo artists are categorised as new school artists. Older generation – old school. The new school artists tend to order their equipment online. Although the equipment has improved, the mentality and tattoo shop professionalism hasn't changed at all.

I have a few years of experience tattooing under my belt nowadays, and the competitive artist co-worker relationship is still a constant frustration. I find this attribute to be a productivity barrier in some tattoo shops and individually believe that the customer encounter and the complete tattoo service should be a main priority.

I learned, coming up from an apprentice to a competent tattoo artist, that the shop rivalry generally stems back to the relationships of the older generation of tattoo artists. The first tattoo shops and their owner's feuds with neighbouring towns tattoo shops and so on. This mindset is passed on and continued. Small feuds and rivalry also continue, with no real basis for the negativity or feud. Yet, as time has gone by, the feuds have also developed, involving a lot of artists that portray negative energy. I have always been amazed by this characteristic.

Artistically natured people can often feel misplaced in modern society and, therefore, find that they can create artistic creations tapping into an energy bought about by this misplacement. Those of that nature strive to fit. And, naturally, their nature is somewhat non-confrontational.

I do not know any good artist that can produce amazing work, when subjected to an unsavoury environment.

As an apprentice, I hadn't considered the underlying negativity. I was blind to it and adored my new career.

But the longer I worked in the tattoo shops, and the more second nature the process became, I discovered I had more time to absorb my surroundings. Therefore, I began noticing shop against shop bickering, artist scandals and negative banter about each other. It created a circulating pot of unhealthy energy. This reminded me of my school days. And as I detested my time at school, I was adamant that I was not going to get caught up.

I took the approach, that if I had nothing good to say, then I wouldn't say anything at all; That I would let my own abilities speak for themselves. I would keep my energy focused on what I wanted to achieve. I never pulled a fellow artist down for their work, and when confronted with other artists doing exactly that to me, I simply pointed out that every artist has room to grow and maybe that is where they should focus their own efforts, rather than on me?

I was of the mind-set that I could make it in my tattoo career. I would find a way to learn what was needed to become a great tattoo artist, and maintain that goal as my primary focus. I intended to keep the industry associations and seedy side of life at an arm's length. Throughout the years, I always felt that I was the unpopular artist amidst the shops I worked in.

My customers loved me and my style of artwork and my bosses have made lots of money off of my work ethic. That was the only negative...I didn't fit with the standard catty crowd. The more I grew as an artist, the more confident I became, and soon, I did not need to be accepted by my co-workers, or succumb to 'the norm' in a tattoo shop. I had a great rapport with customers and always had work...I figured that once my fellow artists grew to know me, that my only intention was to be a good, no, great tattoo artist. That they would understand that I was no threat or hindrance to them. I did not cast judgement their way, nor have a negative word to speak against them, although I had been given plenty of reason.

I maintained a positive focus on my career only, assuming all my responsibilities and providing a consistent superior tattoo service. Maybe I was a threat to them, I just tried to do my job in the best way possible.

I always anticipated that your fellow co-workers would be happy for you as you climbed the apprenticeship ladder. Flourishing into a tattoo artist that they had helped mould... I hoped that there would be a level of camaraderie and encouragement; An underlying connection or bond similar to a family. I hoped to introduce that in my own tattoo shop too.

I am an artist and I don't like confrontation. I would pick a pack of crayons, paper and a good song over people for company any day of the week. Confrontation and hostile working environments stunt my progression. My focus becomes fixed on getting through the day, rather than pushing my artistic skill boundaries. So, I would normally shy away or back down from any artist conflict. There is nothing worse than waking up, hating what you're doing. I had that for most of my childhood. I loathed attending school. That is the reason I picked tattooing as a career. I wanted to love and enjoy what I was doing as a means to earning a living, which is effectively a gigantic portion of your life.

I also wanted to give other people a better experience than what I had. And maybe give someone love for their imperfect body. I want it all to be better for everyone!

17
New job, fresh start and it's summertime

I had closed my tattoo shop and was due to start work overseas. The flight was long but no bother at all. I was looking forward to some nice weather, a new job and attending a tattoo convention in the new town. I had timed the flight, so I could get settled in at the shop and have time to attend the tattoo convention. I love tattoo conventions!

I love the atmosphere, camaraderie and admiration of tattoo art that you and every single stranger attending the convention has in common. *"If you love tattoos and have never attended a convention or tattoo show. Please place it on you 'to-do' list. Jump up on stage and have your five minutes of fame, show your tattoo 'your worldly tattoo family' will love it. You will have a ball)!*

I arrived on a Friday afternoon and had arranged a hire car, so I could drive down to the newly opened tattoo shop's location. I went to the shop in the main town as planned, but when I got there, the shop was closed. I called my boss and she informed me that they had decided to drive down to the new tattoo shop early, and that I should drive down. I did the 3 hour drive to the new shop's location, and although I wasn't sure what to expect, I was still very excited.

When I arrived, I was met with huge disappointment. My new to be boss was annoyed that she was unable to reach me to inform me that they had changed their minds and wanted me to meet them down at the new shop's location. I explained I was on the plane for a long time, that was probably why she couldn't reach me, and driving down to the shop was no hassle for me at all.

I had asked my new boss for help with arranging temporary accommodation near the new shop, at my expense. I did not know the area very well and welcomed her help. She said she would be more than happy to help me sort something. My accommodation had been overlooked and forgotten. I should have known and trusted in that moment, and taken it as a warning sign. A pre-cursor of what to expect. The shop was not well run at all. It looked fantastic on the website. A successful shop with multiple locations and expansion. Sadly, there was no set structure in the new tattoo shop and the multiple tattoo shops were tattoo shops owned by others 'affiliated people' under the same name.

I started work and found that the other artists came and left as and when they pleased. There was there not adequate tattoo furniture at the new location yet either. The artists there were very relaxed and smoked their recreational necessities at the back of the shop. I picked up rapidly that the shop was in fact gang owned, and put my foot in it with one of the biker members at their shop opening day. The owner had assured me that the shop was not biker gang owned, during the 4 phone conversations prior to me accepting the position. And from that I had expressed my delight during a conversation, where I was quickly corrected.

I couldn't see myself settling in here and felt my acceptance of the situation somewhat hypocritical. I had worked too hard to keep a clean slate, free from the gang extortion demands in my own tattoo shop, and with the aim of expanding my career and skills, to find myself working for a gang owned shop now. To me, it meant I had taken 10 steps backwards.

I decided I should move on. I had heard about a region that was about to implement strict regulations around the tattoo industry. There is a big city and lots of contracting tattoo artist positions available.

The tattoo industry regulations due to be implemented were aimed at minimising the gang and biker extortion of tattoo shops.

A much needed clean-up of the popular tattoo industry. I welcomed this change and felt positive about joining a tattoo shop that had no biker gang affiliations or connections, in this area. I was sure that the tattoo shops in this state would be established enough to not have the problems that I have had with my own tattoo shop…Well, I hoped.

I attended the city's tattoo convention, before flying over to the other state.

Walking off the plane, I could feel the region's lovely, warm air. The sun was shining and the world felt bright. I had managed to organise flat share accommodation, prior to leaving.

The lady who shared the house with me was lovely and welcoming. Straight away, I felt relief over my decision to move here.

We lived close to a well-known beach and I was very keen to walk down and have a look around. The sun was beating down and area was very tropical. I loved it!

Walking down the main road toward the beach, I noticed that there was a tattoo shop. To me, tattoo shops stand out like red cars. If you own a red car, that is all you seem to notice. Everywhere you look, red cars spring out at you. Tattoo shops bound out to me. My inner peripheral seems to seek them.

We walked past many shops heading down toward the beach. All of a sudden, I was face to face with a huge tattoo shop. A very well-known one. And as I was looking for a job, I decided to go in and ask if there were any tattoo artist vacancies.

I was met by a big muscly tattooed man with a thunderously loud voice, he bellowed rather than talked, but in a jovial manner. I asked if there were any vacancies and he responded that he was always looking for new talent. I was not prepared at all. I was dressed for the beach and was messily presented. I didn't bring my artist portfolio and didn't have anything to show my tattoo work either.

The big man had an assistant with him, who asked if I had a Facebook page. I told him I did, and how to find it, so they could view my tattoo artwork. Within a couple of minutes, he offered me his bear like hand and gripped my mine. Shaking it, he said, "You've got a job here, girl". I couldn't believe it, I got a job instantly at a renowned tattoo shop...Wow, I felt like the cat that got the cream that afternoon...

I was to start the next day. The shop was very busy and all the artists seemed nice enough. There were a few artists from my home country, they made me feel very welcome.

I was getting into the swing of things at the shop and before I knew it, Christmas was upon us. I had signed up for four days to start with, but that had crept up to six days per week due to seasonal demand. I figured I would make hay whilst hay was to be made...

There wasn't really much time to engage with the other artists, we all kept to ourselves mostly. Some of the long term tattoo artists had established friendships. But I was noticing a divide amongst some people in the shop and I didn't want any part of it. Reflecting on what I had been through prior to moving, I wanted to avoid any encouragement of destructiveness.

The state had new regulations introduced for tattoo artists and tattoo shop owners.

We all required licenses and had to submit forms to prove, that as individuals, we are not associated or linked with biker gangs. I had applied for mine as soon as I planned to go to the state. The regulations were to help eliminate the gangs or bikers from making money through owning the tattoo shops, or forcing tattoo shop owners to pay monies to the regional biker gangs. It was exactly the same as my small country. Tattoo shops are split into areas, regions or territories. A particular gang or biker group may have dibs or ownership of that particular region and that is where their tattoo shops operate from. Even if tattoo shops are owned independently, the biker gang will ensure that you pay them to operate in their region. They run tattoo shops in their designated area and trade in cash payments for the tattoo services. Tattoo shops are very lucrative to the biker gangs and are used as a main source of income.

Tattoo artists are hired as contractors and are paid in a cash percentages. The tattoo artists provide the services to the public, but work for the tattoo shop as a house.

Running the operation in cash has many benefits. Cash avoids taxations and employment remunerations and fees that go along with legitimately run businesses. Any person who chooses to open a tattoo shop usually finds themselves in the following predicament: They are visited by the regional gang or biker group, who has ownership of that area.

The visit will end up with one of the two outcomes. The new tattoo shop owners agrees to pay a percentage payment to the gang and is allowed to operate in the area. Or the tattoo shop is closed down by the biker gang!

With new regulations in place, I am hopeful that there will be a change in the type of people who own tattoo shops.

A new wave of shop ownership along with professional regulations and operation standards. A safer environment for contractors, and a more stable remunerative contracting or employment process will hopefully follow.

Tattoo artists are the worker ants of the industry. We are on the bottom of the food chain. To the world, a career as a tattoo artist seems luxurious and grandiose. Little work for a lucrative income and a fashionable reputed field to work in.

The monetary service fees are paid mostly to the house or the shop's regional affiliations or biker gang.

I am hoping, that by explaining, this book will educate the public on the amount of work a good tattoo artist undergoes for the customer. And promote positive thoughts around possible improvements to the working environments of contracting tattoo artists.

I am pro-change and can't wait for this legislation to be executed everywhere! Including my hometown...

I understand that the industry once belonged to an older generation, and tattoos are linked to the sordid side of life. However, we live in a much more evolved world today. And customer service and employer considerations are priorities in businesses. The tattoo service is a business and, therefore, should be regulated accordingly.

I personally embraced tattooing passionately as a career choice. I wasn't privy to the knowledge of gang, biker regional ownership and their involvement. I did not know what extortion meant, nor did I have any idea about the enforcement actions taken by the bike gangs.

If I had been educated to how calculated, callous, and inhumane the conduct initiated by these money-driven Neanderthals could be, I would have never chosen this career path.

Once you develop as a tattoo artist, and grow beyond the 'popularity' of the profession, you becomes service oriented and artistically driven. You gain a desire to bring more to your own service and care more about the tattoo artwork you provide.

Many artists share my frustration with the unprofessional and illegitimate ways in which the tattoo shops are run. And these new regulations open up a huge opportunity for change.

I hope to embrace it, promote new concepts and ways of thinking in the tattoo industry.

The hierarchal, chauvinist ego that so many tattoo artists harbour serves no purpose in a shop. The macho dominance and intimidating conduct of the purely money driven owners also serves no purpose in a tattoo shop.

The tattoo shop provides an artistic service. The tattoo artists are service providers. They and the customers should be the number one concern. The artistic service that is to be provided to the customer.

Real artists care! We care a lot and have a gift. We will spend hours fine tuning a tattoo design for a customer, most of the time, at our own expense. We are not necessarily competitive. Our best work is extracted when we are at ease. We aim to please. And if asked to choose between the passions of our artwork compared to money, most of us choose the art work every time.

Of course, I can't speak for everyone, but many artists I have met along the way share the same anxieties as I. Some of us would like to own our own tattoo shop, or like I, actually be able to give it a go without the intimidation, threats and stand over actions from the territorial gangs and rough bikers.

The shop owners who allow association and condone the extortion payments have no consideration for their staff or their customers. MONEY is the driving force for those tattoo shops.

The shop I had joined was a tattoo sweatshop. After the novelty of the new popular location had worn off, I realised that my artistic goal would also not come to fruition in a tattoo shop of this nature. We were pushed to do fast turnaround tattoos. Large tattoo pieces and project tattoo pieces were not considered, unless the customer was happy to pay the full price per hour. The hours were colossal and rather than being a great tattoo artist, I was a tired numb copy machine. I may as well have been making sport shoes.

And yet again, although the owner assured me that the shop was not associated, we still had the patched thugs coming into the shop for their fortnightly payments. So that was a load of bull!

When you have worked in a few shops, you get to know what's what. You are not blind and can visibly understand what is going on… Shops are just shifting the ownership and operational licenses over to their partners, friends or artists that 'look' clean and not associated. When in fact they are.

So, after a long summer, it was time to push forward and try and find the shop that I was meant to be a part of.

The team I was to join would be where I would grow and feel proud of my artistic achievements again...theme song, *"Here I go again on my own..."*

Maybe, I should just open another tattoo shop myself? Mmm...

18

Small town tattoo shop, is this where I am meant to be?

There are tons of tattoo artist vacancies in this state, and after searching for a couple of days, I found one where I thought I may fit. I expressed my anxieties about the biker and gang affiliations to the shop owner. I made it very clear, that if the shop was connected, I would not settle there and would be wasting their time.

I accepted the position once offered and left my current shop. I was sad to leave the location, as I loved the beach.

But I knew I would have to try a few shops until I found the right one…The morning started out as a good day. I went into work to get set up for my first days client. You learn to work to a certain level of autonomy as a contracting tattoo artist. I had grown used to bumbling around in my own little world, before after and during clients.

Anyway, 'Miss Feral', supposedly our shop manager, was in early and giving someone a severe roasting down the phone when I arrived. This conversation carried on for a few minutes. The shop atmosphere was very cold, a direct reflection of the controversial phone conversation. The pessimistic vibe that had been created set the mood for the day. As I looked around, I figured all of us artists were dreading the day that we had ahead of us. Even the new guy, who had just come back to work at the shop after having some personal stress leave. He said to me, "Is she always like this?" to which I replied, "I have only been here for a couple of days, yes mate, I think so".

I knew from the pit of my stomach that I would be Miss Feral's target that day. I'd learned she'd had been through a rough time at a previous shop and was kicked to curb. The boss of that shop had been influenced by a female co-worker artist. There was the motive.

I am a competent tattoo artist. I still have a huge way to go to get to where I am aiming as an artist. But my current ability gives me confidence to walk into any tattoo shop and provide a good level of tattoo art as a service.

I am very head strong, knowing my job perimeters and expectations.

Miss Feral and I clashed. To educate the reader, when you join a new shop, there is a certain amount of standing your ground that has to be established. This is classed as a tattoo shop dynamic. This changes when new a tattoo artist comes or when one leaves. Artists establish who is who and often who the shop pushover is will also be determined. I have a level of respect that I bring to the table, no matter where I work. I communicate that I have mutual respect and an expectation that the same is returned. Most artists are relieved when you are nice and relaxed. But some will push your boundaries to see how far they can take you. I still haven't come up with a formula for joining a new shop yet. And often fly by the seat of my pants...I pray a lot to work with nice artists.

I had tried to reassure Miss Feral that I was not after her job or her departure, my intentions lie within the boundaries of tattooing; working in the tattoo shop as a contracting artist and providing a tattoo service...no more. I had no interest in running a shop, even though I could do a far better job of it than she could. *"Even with my eyes closed"*.

We had a couple of personal chats before this confrontational day, trying to come to terms with our individual, strong personalities. This is where I learned that she had been burned. She also made me aware that the girls in this tattoo shop only work for one 'club'.

Club meaning gang. You guessed it. You have got to be kidding me. Maybe I should just 'suck-it-up' save up and re-open another tattoo shop myself...I definitely thought my expectations were way too high. Maybe acceptance of this was the way things needed to be right now...

Miss Feral educated me that the girls who worked at this shop were true to that particular gang. And wouldn't work for any other tattoo shop or biker gang. That other artists were considered dogs for swapping shops. Gang associated tattoo shops. And of course, this information was delivered in the best-spoken use of the English language. Internally, I had a giggle to myself; this chick was pretty rough alright, and she wouldn't need to lay a hand on anyone. Her hostile word projection of 'F...ing dogs' was spat off of her tongue like projectile bullet. And the words would hit and hurt whoever aimed at, for sure!

I had a completely different perspective. I tried to explain that I had no loyalties to any particular biker gang and never would. My focus was one hundred percent on my tattoo artwork. My provided service and skill set 'growth' was my goal and intention.

This went completely over her head. I was shut down by her what's the point attitude. I talked to her about my frustrations about the gang owned tattoo shops. She had been through a pretty rough time herself. I explained that I was focused on providing a great tattoo service to the public and conducting myself as a professional, raising the bar and pushing my own artistic abilities. As I hoped to be a renowned great tattoo artist someday...

I think our chat divided us more than it mended any personality differences. So, I knew Miss Feral would be gunning for me at some point. But I didn't expect it to be so soon.

During her dramatic phone conversation, she threw around the use of her contacts being the bikers associated with this tattoo shop. She was still threatening her caller, when the daily customers started to filter in. Realising how unprofessional she looked, Miss Feral wrapped her phone conversation up. Her focus was then back on the shop.

You may at this stage be asking yourself why I was still around. Now that I was fully aware that the tattoo shop was gang owned. The reason is I had been started on two very large tattoos, a sleeve and a chest piece. One unwritten rule with tattoo shops. You do not start and leave with large unfinished tattoo pieces. You never know what is around the corner or when you'll need a job. And although the shop owner gang and rivals may not get along, the shops know who's who and who is doing what. So a bad rep will travel. I also consider the customer and want to honor any tattoo work that I started with their best experience at the forefront of my considerations. Unless the customer is really hard to work with or is problematic. Then they can find another artist as some people you just cannot please. All in all I have a pretty good name apart from not wanting to work for an affiliated tattoo shop.

I had been left on my own to close the tattoo shop the previous day, and as I hadn't had any training on the exact process for this shop, I had used my initiative and made a note of all the details. I aimed to total the takings the following day, when someone could advise me how.

First, I was accused as to where the money was. I had placed it in the till but in the incorrect area. Then, I was spat at for closing the shop. NO – hey, thanks for staying back when all the other lazy artists left early. Or – I noticed that you emptied the bins, vacuumed and washed the floors before you left. Thanks for that...Which was her complaint the previous day.

When she spat at me, I responded in a 'quiet' tone, which resulted in her losing her constitution at me. I was called a lot of very nice names. I was told I was not be trusted, that I was a female dog...And all of this was in front of my co-workers and customer, who was sat in the lounge area. Disgusting!

So you can imagine what the rest of the day was like...This was my first week of starting a new job in a professional environment a tattoo shop supposedly ran like a hair salon... This was appalling! I applied for the job by replying to an internet job site; Contracting tattoo artist in a nice town, change of scenery. A two year old tattoo shop, run similarly to a hair salon, in a professional and friendly environment with predominantly female artists...Sounds lovely, doesn't it? I thought so too. What a load of bollox!

The owner and I had come up with a game plan. I set in stone that her conduct was not tolerable and that I was more than happy to seek work elsewhere. I would work anywhere else, rather than wake up each morning with dread as to what unprofessional events the feral shop manager may bring that day. And yes, she managed the entire shop, I could not believe this either. There also wasn't as much work in that town. A back log of two months' work was promised. There wasn't much work at all. I had now subscribed to working three days a week, opposite to the days Miss Feral worked. This was for smoother working conditions, can you believe this? Until my large pieces had been completed. Then I would be leaving.

The owner informed me that the last female tattoo artist was bullied into leaving and she would like me to consider staying.

I have zero tolerance for bulling; whether I am intended to be the receiver or another person is. I will squash it dead with whatever means necessary. In my older age, I'd prefer a more subtle manner of resolving conflict, but make no mistake, I will never tolerate bullying in my life again. Ever!

I choose to have a calm, level-headed, friendly and approachable personality; however, there is a line! Adults develop from their experiences and negative occurrences during childhood can often lead to poor or instinctive decisions as an adult. Everyone was bullied at some stage of their life, I received my fair share and possibly your share too, if you didn't get bullied. There came a day where I decided no more, and no matter how big the bully or number of people, I would stand up to them and fight with everything I had...I had nothing to lose. And NO-ONE could hurt me any more than what had already been done.

I'm not sure who is scarier? The people doing the bullying, or the person who has nothing left to loose. You get my point!

So, I was in a great predicament. Not only had I uprooted myself to a small town to start a new tattoo job that didn't have full time work, that had actually turned out to be gang owned and now I had to sought work elsewhere.

I find a ton of work and gave another shop a go outside of the city back toward the beach. And to place the icing on the cake, this tattoo shop was also owned by another biker gang. Except this biker gang happened to be rivals of the small town owned tattoo shop where I was currently working. *"Are you serious, I think I need a whiskey...?"*

A few weeks later, I had a gut full of the unprofessionally run small town tattoo shop. I couldn't do another day of waking up and dreading what work 'dramas' would unfold. My last session of one of the larger tattoos I have under took was due in and that would neatly wrap up my contract artist services. So, I handed in my notice to both biker gang owned tattoo shops. I did not want to subscribe to being a part of any affiliated tattoo shop, if I had a choice.

I had given notice to the town tattoo shop. I explained that I wanted to move back to the beach and that I was struggling with the association.

I made brief chitchat with my co-worker artists about my plans. I suggested that I intended to join a new team near the beach, that had no connections at all. A few girls had gotten together, we all shared the same struggles in the tattoo industry. They knew my work and offered me a position. I explained that we were a group of tattooists, that had come together, and wanted to provide tattoos without any hindrances from gangs or bikers.

The co-workers asked me who was backing the shop. This meant which gang was supporting the tattoo shop or taking payments. New shops needed a biker gang to 'protect' them. Again, this meant paying the territory biker gang extortion money and the crappy circle would continue.

I asked what they meant by backing the new shop that I intended to work from. They implied that that territory where the shop is located was owned by one gang. And that gang would not allow any independently owned tattoo shop to be operating in their region. The co-workers mentioned that this particular gang was known to have the worst reputation and has carried out some very bad actions toward non-compliant tattoo shop owners and their artists.

I explained to my co-workers that we were a few family oriented artists. We intended to keep a low key persona. And that none of us were out to cause any trouble, we just didn't want to be associated with any biker gang members or work for any biker gangs owned tattoo shops anymore.

I had left my home country and closed my tattoo shop, with the aim of joining a good tattoo shop with great artists and a more professional environment. I intend to advance my tattooing skills and further my career. And with the new regulations that are being implemented here in this state, I was sure that the tattoo industry could offer that.

There were a few ladies who were fantastic artists, and who had already grouped together and opened a tattoo shop. We enquired if they had biker backing, and it seemed like they had been allowed to continue their professional tattoo shop with no extortion. This may have been the pioneering tattoo shop and we hoped to follow in their footsteps.

Yes, more – Artist Owned Independent Professional Tattoo Shops.

I have been warned by current co-workers, who were familiar with the territory's gang and their customs, that we were enticing and encouraging the stand over actions. The shop could be burned down or shot at. The shop could be broken into and all our equipment stolen. We could be beaten and have our hands broken, so that we would be unable to work. They could even shoot an artist...All of the above had happened before in that state. I was sure that I would be the first to be targeted, if anything did come about. My personality was flamboyant and I naturally attracted customers. I also loved and participated in shows and events, promoting my services wherever I could.

I also did not hide that I did not support biker owned tattoo shops and had made this clear to a couple of tattoo shops when applying for vacancies.

I had been at war with myself for many years.

"Maybe I should accept that this is the way of tattoo shops. Maybe I should jump on board with this way of life and not try to make any service improvements. Maybe I should care less about my co-workers and other contracting artists. Maybe I should care less for my customers and the services they receive? By lowering my standards and

expectations of myself... Maybe I should accept my place in life...

Why am I here and why have I gone through what I have? Why was I bought up strong, with a natural desire to help others? If I give up the expectations for myself, then I give up the want and desire to be a better person. Once that is taken away...

What is the point?

Because I don't know." And that is why I have written this book.

19

Can we make it better for contracting tattoo artists and the Joe Public?

Tattoo shops are currently under the magnifying glass in this state. The state regulations are expected to be upheld, or tattoo shop owners will face the consequences handed out by authorities. So, there is a big change in the way tattoo shops are conducted. There are many opinions on whether or not the changes to the industry are positive. Here are some of the encounters I have had been exposed to as a contracting artist. And to be honest if the changes promote better working environments, and provide improved levels of service, then I don't see any harm in the regulations. And, in fact, I am on board with them.

I have worked in a shop where one of the younger artists supported the affiliated biker members owning the tattoo shop. As a motorcycle from another biker association was driven past the front shop window, the artist was sitting in plain view and pulled finger gestures at the passing motorcyclists. I was working on a customer at this time, the customer was someone who had been referred to me and not a customer of the shop. The artist then continued to run down the particular association of the passing rider, using profound and absurd language. All whilst I was working on a member of the public. So, not only was the public subjected to unspeakable behaviour during their service, but as a contracting artist, I was endangered, categorised and labelled to be onside with that specific tattoo shop. As a contracting artist, I consider this to be absurd. I was placed in a compromising and dangerous predicament. I had been hired as a contracting tattoo artist, with the intent of providing a tattoo service.

My customer was disgusted by my fellow artist's conduct and I had to discount her total tattoo cost for the embarrassing service. Not only did I lose a customer while I operated from that tattoo shop, but I was seen or assumed to subscribe to this shop and their gang association. Only because I was working there as a contractor tattoo artist.

When, in actual fact, I do not subscribe to or condone any gang, association or biker group. I merely work as a contracting tattoo artist at licensed tattoo shops. The business of which, sadly, the biker gangs have monopoly over.

Another experience I had, was with a large and renowned tattoo shop. The shop had a large number of contracting artists and had a very large clientele base during the summer season. This shop conducted over half a year's work, without addressing the sterilising process and standards in the shop. I witnessed a myriad of stainless steel tubes, that had not had their rubber sleeves removed prior to any cleaning. These tubes were covered with rust, discolouration and metal deterioration. And yet, they were bagged, autoclaved and re-used, week after week.

Another shop had an autoclave that had a fault and was discontinued. So, rather than organising the autoclave to be repaired, which should be done annually, they stopped using it. Only pulsing the stainless tubes in the pulse steriliser, rinsing and reusing them...

Other shops haven't had autoclaves and claimed that they relied on disposable systems and yet they would perform piercings using stainless steel clamps, which are not disposable. These items did need to be sterilised and autoclaved.

The public, who do not have a clear understanding with regard to what is expected around cross contamination hazards in a tattoo shops, rely and place trust in the tattoo businesses to provide a safe service.

To the Joe Public, I urge you to educate yourself and ask questions. Make sure the shop you are attending is providing the correct procedure when performing a tattoo and or piercing. And that they are using correctly sterilised equipment and processes.

Shops with a high turnover can be complacent. Sterilising processes and limited materials may be favoured for the monetary gain over the customer's welfare.

Shops will ask you to sign your disclaimer or consent form prior to any consultation or tattoo performance preparation. You will likely sign the form in the waiting room, before your tattoo or piercing service has commenced.

Once you have signed the form, you have assumed the full responsibility and liability of that procedure. And, sadly, in the worst case scenario, you will not be able to pinpoint any contamination to that procedure.

Also, I would like to make the point that the customer has a choice. Intimidation and badgering to influence customers' haste, when making a decision about a tattoo, is not acceptable. You, the customer, should not be made to feel like you are rushed or have limited options. However, considerations are advised for pre-booked tattoos. This is basic tattoo etiquette for your artist. Your artist may have organised and taken your design request prior to your booking date. If this is the case, then it is courteous to contact your artist, if you intend to make design changes prior to your booking time.

Your tattoo artist will educate you and offer advice about your tattoo design, and about what looks aesthetically appealing when placing your tattoo design on your body. Size also influences the detail of the tattoo. Your artist will explain how a tattoo ink heals, relaxes, and settles into the skin. Small lettering may have limitations, as the skins area elasticity may determine the minimum size, especially when working with small lettering fonts.

There isn't adequate policing to insure that correct sterilisation processes are being followed by every tattoo artist. Shop management does seem more concerned with the amount of tattoos performed, above tattoos that are performed correctly. Hopefully, we will see some upgrades in this area.

I have found that there is no process in place for contractors. Contracting tattoo artists and the expectations of them is a 'large grey area'. Each tattoo shop's processes may differ and there are no set regulations around the rights of contracting tattoo artists.

Since the regulations have been put into operation, we contractor tattoo artists are to be state licensed and provide services to the house or shop, as a licensed premise, to operate from.

The houses or shops that host the contractors have no structure or guidelines. The old school way of splitting the cash remunerations for each tattoo performed is to split the total cost of the tattoo into a percentage. This doesn't necessarily work well today for the contracting artist. GST and Superannuation is now enforced, and tattoo businesses are expected to manage their accounts correctly. Some shops pay GST that is deducted from the service fee, as well as claim the GST from the artist's percentage. The aim is that the GST is to be paid for the contracting artist by the house or shop, portraying consideration for the contracting artist. Where in fact, the GST money from the artist's invoice gets pocketed to boost the tattoo shops earnings. This is also done for Superannuation and Workers compensation. Two areas where the tattoo shops can claim monetary amounts from the contracting artist's remuneration percentages. And heaven forbid, if you leave or get fired from the shop. As the GST, Superannuation and Workers' Compensation amounts taken from the artist remunerations is not paid to the correct organisations and does not get paid on their behalf of the contracting artist either. Never Paid!

Enforcing the payments and going up against these types of people, once the artist has left the shop, can result in abuse, threats or no-work in the entire region. Tattoo artists find themselves in a predicament, where they have no influence, and therefore, do nothing.

Tattoo shop materials and who supplies what is also a huge grey area. Most shops provide the miscellaneous cleaning items and sterilising equipment. They must house the correct licenses or health department approval certificates. Premises and suitable tattoo furniture also needs to be provided. The artist is to supply their tattoo ink, needles, tattoo machines, power supply and some miscellaneous consumables. This works, as long as the shop maintains their stock.

In many cases, tattoo artists stock their entire process materials and are not considered for any monetary reimbursement...

There are concerns of liabilities. The tattoo shop or house generally keep the disclaimers and do not offer or allow the contracting artist to obtain copies. The reason for this is competition and access to the client's information that is detailed in the disclaimer. But who is responsible for poorly performed tattoos, pigment reactions and worse – contracted infections? The house or the artist?

Also, with artists expected to bring in clientele for the businesses, surely the disclaimers are the property of the service provider? Which is the contracting artist, so it is quite possibly necessary for liability insurances, which the housing shop will urge the contracting artist obtain themselves.

Possibly, it should be the shop that is insured for public liability. And which should have policies and procedures in place for accurate services to be provided...

Tattoo pigment or ink has a life too and should be replaced regularly. Correct and safe tattoo pigments have health numbers and information detailing their usability. Some inks are organic and others do contain ingredients that some people will react to.

If the shop does not provide the correct usable materials, most of the time, the reason is money-saving and cost cutting. How do you ensure your contracting artist is providing the adequate services and using the correct cleaning and sterilising methods in the shop. At the moment, there isn't anything in place to insure that.

I would also consider that health departments and authorisations have a hard time going into tattoo shops to enforce correct ethics.

If the tattoo shops are happy to intimidate disgruntled customers that may have legitimate complaints about a service, or contracting staff that may question the unfair boundaries, then what chance do governing health enforcers have?

I have worked in tattoo shops, where the artist's remunerations are tampered with, are inconsistent and additional deductions are created, so that the shop can keep more of the money. Tattoo artists are penalised with monetary penalties, dictated to about increased hours and jobs, and threatened when trying to address any areas of concern.

I have witnessed management belittling, stand overs, abuse, fights and disgusting conduct, whilst trying to provide a service as a contracting tattoo artist to a member of the public.

Contracting artists are also expected to self-promote and gain more work by advertising on social media by handing out flyers and business cards for the shop that we contract to. We are only allowed to contract to one shop at one time, and nine times out of ten, have our work hours dictated to us.

There is no consideration to the contracting artist, their customers or family. The shop claims ownership of the contractor's clientele, when in fact, the clientele builds rapport with the tattoo artist and will stay with an artist if they are happy with their service.

The customer may not have anything to do with the shop at all and chooses the contracting artists style of tattooing. The relationship thread is between the customer and the artist in most situations.

Yet, contracting artists are easily disposable and are disposed of or fired if we question or push back against areas we may disagree with.

I have watched artist's trolleys, containing their equipment, being rolled outside of the shop and dismissed without genuine reason. Purely for standing up against a process that was not correct. There was no consideration for the family of the artist, nor the time of year, as the artist was fired two weeks before Christmas. It bought me to tears, how this artist was treated and disposed of like a used piece of rubbish.

This tattoo shop's owners had little management ethics and zero communication skills. Sadly, this is a regular occurrence in tattoo shops, leaving no room for effective communication between artists and management, or for remedies, when problems arise.

At this particular shop, I had my Superannuation deducted and never paid, and although I chased up the amount owed, I was unable to enforce payments of my deducted superannuation due to who these shop owners are, and who they are connected with. It was best to leave things alone and not make any waves, I was advised.

So, where does that leave the contracting artist, or me? Does that mean I have to pay the amount that has already been deducted from my percentage remuneration? If I the artist does not pay the owed superannuation amount, where does the non-payment leave the artist with the expected requirements in this state?

Again, the contracting tattoo artist struggles to be an obligatory member of society.

Some food for thought: Application of a tattoo artist's position could start with a detailed Curriculum Vitae, containing the contracting tattoo artist's work history, skill sets, and specialty. Their availability and how they see themselves as an additional service provider in the tattoo shop could be detailed. Specifics around the information of licensing and cross-contamination education should also be provided, and a portfolio of drawings and performed tattoos.

The artist's career, attributes, goals, and how they see themselves as an asset to the industry, could be described. There could also be details of their artistic capabilities, preferred genres and their own their point of difference in comparison to other artists…Also, how and where they see themselves in a few years' time...

On a more professional level, the tattoo company would then meet with the artist, providing they are an eligible candidate for the contracting tattoo artist position. Maybe a possible demonstration could be arranged to assess how the artist conducts their station and client management.

A further meeting after the assessment would address any areas of concern. This would include an induction into how the tattoo shop operates, education regarding the tattoo shop policies and procedures, and a discussion around the work hours and availability.

Adequate remunerations, based on the artist's ability, would be agreed upon. Set details on liabilities around taxes and superannuation's would also be defined. A term and contract would be presented and signed.

Definition around the ownership of performed tattoo art work should be agreed. When a contracting tattoo artist moves on from a tattoo shop, the promotion of their performed tattoo work in that shop should be allowed to be advertised by that artist, as additions to their portfolio. This image gallery may be online, on social media, and a website or photo book. At the moment, some shops can bully and claim ownership of the tattoo work performed at their shop.

Two areas to consider here: Firstly, the tattoo artist is expected to network, gain their own customers and promote their own style of art work.

Secondly, the shop takes the remunerative percentage and, quite possibly, may not be able to replicate or provide that exact artist's tattoo style. The tattoo contractor's portfolio demonstrates what tattoo work the artist can provide, and their artwork style.

Which, in my eyes, belongs to the artist. There is no contract signed for intellectual property and the tattoo shop is not publicised in any way. The portfolio specifically demonstrates the tattoo skill and artistic ability of the individual contracting tattoo artist.

If a working contract was offered to a contracting tattoo artist, it would not only explain the expectation of the contracting artist, but it would secure the subscription of the expectation from the contracting tattoo artist to the tattoo shop. The contract would commit the contracting tattoo artist to a work or employment time frame.

This would benefit the contracting tattoo artist considerably!

At the moment, tattoo artists are not considered functional members of society, we are paid in cash and given no commitment to a working time periods. This means we are ineligible for loans, unable to create credit ratings or apply for mortgages. We are deemed to have no secure means of income, in the eyes of lending organisations. This is a cycle, as it puts pressure on some artists to gain financial capital using unorthodox methods. Some methods are inspired by the unsavoury characters that own the tattoo shops, which are the associated with the biker gangs...

Artist should be able to manage their own 'negotiated' remunerations, pay their own GST, Workers compensation and Superannuation. The tattoo shop or housing company should have the liabilities clearly defined in the contracting artist's contract.

The artists should be able to have their invoiced remuneration paid into their banking accounts, rather than being paid in cash wads each week.

And tattoo shops should have business banking accounts and provide electronic banking payment options. We all seem to send clients off to ATM's to withdraw cash amounts when they arrive for their tattoo. This request is rather archaic in this day and age.

Contracting artists should be able to get affordable tattoo artist's insurance and work with the tattoo shop owners to ensure adequate services are provided. Remedies for unsatisfied customers should also be managed with the customers' focus at the forefront.

I am hoping to promote thought and possibly positive change for contracting tattoo artist. Contractor or employment positions applied for by artists should be in a similar format as any other business professionals. And remuneration should be based on the skill and the experience of the contracting tattoo artist... Food for thought.

20
Attempting to negotiate a mutual understanding

The new shop is amazing. I bounce out of bed in the mornings and really look forward to what the day may bring. My fellow co-workers artists are lovely. I consider myself very blessed to be surrounded by such beautiful artistic people.

The small shop is now open, and we have a huge task on our hands of marketing and creating bookings. I had an offer of a couple of trade stalls at the city events. The events are not directly involved with tattooing, but they attract lots of different people. And for the price of their trade site, setting up and promoting the shop couldn't hurt...So, we're going to give it a go.

We are all excited but nervous at the same time. We want to promote the tattoo shop, without creating any tension or unwanted attention from the biker gangs that own the other tattoo shops. So, attending one of the fashion marquees and having a stall that displays our art work, as well as our tattoo work, is a bit nerve wracking. The weekend came about and the weather gods had granted us a fantastic day. Complete sunshine and not a cloud in sight. We were all up at the crack of dawn. We had a huge day ahead of us and didn't really know what to expect. We were on time for our trade site loading and managed to set up the stall quite quickly. This gave us an hour to grab a coffee, before the Fashion Marquee opened. For some reason, coffee tastes the absolute best when you have it at a crazily early hour in the morning.

The first few people filtered through after the event had opened. I must admit, we all stood there like goldfish to start with. Once we had approached a couple of browsing people, chatting to the public became easier. We had good feedback and found that most people had enquiries and questions about tattoos, but would never go into a tattoo shop to gain the information. We managed to give out lots of business cards. The whole day worked out well with only one little hiccup.

It was a little after lunch, and I was one of the two that was to take the first afternoon shift at our trade stall. The other was walking around, mixing with the general public. I had been to grab a bite to eat and was feeling ready to get out there and promote the little tattoo shop again. As I did, and started chatting to a couple of passers-by, I noticed a couple of leather vested men out of the corner of my eye. As soon as I saw them, I was alert to their presence. I was surprised to see the bikers at the event. They were definitely biker members, their vests did not display their patches and were clear of any insignia advertising as to who they were. But, I figured they were bikers. I knew I was right after a few minutes and was sure they had spotted our trade stand. The men bee-lined straight for us. I was looking at one of the men and didn't want to break eye contact. They both walked briskly toward our trade site. The other general public were sort of meandering at a slow place through the marquee. The bikers walking pace stood out.

I didn't want to drop eye contact with the man, as this may have shown them that I was nervous and scarred. I stood tall, smiled at the leather clad men and asked them how their morning was, and if they like the event? Inside, I felt a tense knot in my stomach and my brain was going overtime. My mouth wouldn't...Shut up. I gave them the sales pitch I gave everyone else and handed them a card. They left and I think they were as taken aback as I...

The event ended up being a great success and we had made a few connections for tattoo work. Everyone had put in a huge effort, the day was good but tiring and it was great to get home.

The next few weeks were routine again. We were working away on a few clients and were considering other advertising avenues. The Marquee was very inexpensive compared to some of the large shows and only really expended effort and energy. We collaborated and decided that we would do a couple more small events, similar to what we had done.

That evening, I had my usual Friday evening customer. He was getting a large biblical back tattoo and booked with me every second Friday evening. One of the other girls was working as well. She was doing a tattoo on one of her friends, I think. Around 7.45pm, we had a knock at the door. We thought nothing of it, as the shop stays open until 9pm.

It was the leather vested guy, who I had spoken to at the event. My stomach knotted instantly. I was expecting some form of backlash from the bikers that owned the other tattoo shops in the area. But, this evening, I felt caught off guard.

Everything seemed to be running so smoothly, and as time went by, I thought that the biker may not be too bothered by us and our little tattoo shop. I hoped and prayed that this would be the case, to be honest.

I opened the door and could hardly talk. A bit different than when I engaged with him at the Fashion Marquee event, where my mouth wouldn't stop chattering. I remember him clear as day. Under different circumstances, I would find him very attractive. He had mid length sandy blond hair with a blonde / tangerine tinged beard and mo. He stood a least 6ft 1" and was medium build. His friend, I didn't take too much notice of, his look was kind of weasel-like. I admit the biker was good-looking. I have been through enough in the past, and do not want to re-live any of it,. I firmly refuse to entertain any form of attraction toward anyone that is associated or connected with bikers or the biker lifestyle. I assume full responsibility for my future and will not encounter those experiences again.

The good-looking sandy haired biker asked about a tattoo and the costs at our shop. I politely answered that the cost was based on the design. Once we had organised the design and size, we could then provide a cost quotation. The biker had a look around, and while he did, I finished up with my customer. I patched up the tattooed area I had been working on and gave my customer his aftercare. We rebooked for two weeks and settled the payment. My customer then departed and I focused my energy on Mr Biker again.

Rather than beating about the bush, I confronted the situation and asked him outright if his intentions were to persuade us into paying weekly percentages of money to the biker association he was connected with. He laughed at me and looked down at his boots. He nodded, looked up and said, "Yup!" I asked to speak to him outside, as there was other people in the shop and I didn't want to subject them to any of this bother.

I diplomatically asked if he minded if I spoke candidly with him and made sure he was aware that I intended no disrespect in any way.

"The way I currently see the present situation is: We have set up our own shop to provide a specialised tattoo service to the public. We all work part time jobs doing addition menial tasks for remunerations. This enables us to concentrate on the quality of the tattoo art work we are providing. We are not a big shop and do not intended on becoming a big tattoo shop. We do not provide fast turnaround tattoos and would not be much of a monetary asset to the biker gang. So, can you please take this into consideration?

On the flip side, all of us are at a stage in our lives where we are prepared to stand up and fight. We all have been working in the tattoo industry for many years and have complete knowledge on how badly shops operate. We do not and will not subscribe to that way of service.

You also may like to consider that the regional state police have implemented regulations around the tattoo industry. And it seems that the bikers and biker gangs are under the microscope at the moment. The police do not need to be given any reason to execute further regulations, or even stop biker owned tattoo parlours from operating.

And if your biker gang carries out tactics of intimidation, and tries to enforce our little tattoo shop to close, or pay you, then we intend to fight back. Between us, we have enough industry knowledge and know-how of who's who and connect with which shop. That if a single hair is hurt on anyone's head that is connected directly to us. The media, social media, police and fair trading will receive full statements and details. Giving the authorities ammunition to take action against you guys.

We mean no disrespect. We want to stay safe and earn a living doing tattoo art as a service and in return. Your biker gang stays out of the spotlight and leave us alone, how does that sound".

He didn't look at me at all while I was talking to him, whereas, before, he looked me in the eyes. This is the first sign that a man is carrying out something he really doesn't want to be doing. They cannot look you in the eye, and this made me nervous. He just did a head nod acknowledgment and walked away.

I'm thinking, okay? Is that okay, I'll talk to the bikers? Okay, we'll leave you alone? Okay, were going to gun down or burn your shop. Okay, were going to grab one of you and bash you to a pulp until you agree to pay us? What does the nod mean...?

I frantically blurted out:

"I mean it! You can take my life away, I personally won't back down". And as if those words would add any great weight...

"Oh my gosh, Jaimie. Will you shut up" – my inside voice was yelling at me. I walked back inside, feeling shaken. I relayed the details to everyone else and we set up some contingencies for the worst case scenario. This is pretty scary and I'm not sure these ladies really know what them may be in for…

I was on tenterhooks for a few weeks and expected a response of some sort from the biker gang, who sent the bikers around to our tattoo shop. I didn't know their identity by viewing their insignia. I just knew who the local territory 'belonged' to, so I assumed it was that gang.

It must have been four weeks to the day, as I had my back piece in again that Friday night. We did an extra hour that night, so I didn't leave the shop until 9pm. When I locked up the door ready to go home, I felt as though I was being watched. I turned around and saw Mr blond Biker walking toward me. Oh shit, here we go, I thought to myself. Instantly, my stomach knotted, my mouth dried and heart started pounding. I knew it. A mutual understanding...Who am I kidding?

He walked up close to me, real close. Past the invisible 'my space to your space' line. Invasion of privacy, close. I was trembling by now, but managed to say, "Hey how's it going?" I was praying I portrayed no fear, even though I was freaking out inside!

He smelled like whiskey, cigarettes and leather...I know that smell oh so well, at one time in my life, I liked that smell. Now, it makes me retch every time I smell it. It takes me right back instantly to unsavory memories.

He was so close, I could smell his wiry beard. My nose came to the bottom of it, he was quite tall. By this time, I was shaking like a leaf. My trembles had turned almost to convulsions and I was sure I was going to be severely hurt. I was clutching my laptop bag and remembering how a man on the news fought off an attacker with his laptop. He had avoided getting a mallet to his head, I was thinking...Maybe I could do the same?

There was no-one around at this time. He must have waited around. I had finished late tonight and he wouldn't have known that. My senses were heightened, the air felt thick and unable to inhale. I was looking for a sign of his intentions, a knife, a gun... Anything. Any glimpse could help me think of a way to defend myself... Time stood still. The dark seemed really dark. OH god, what had we done?

I was expecting Mr Biker to pull out a knife and plunge it into me, cut my hand so I couldn't work or do something that would hinder me driving the direction of the shop. That was the reason why he had come so close toward me...Or fire a gun into my stomach, muffling the sound as much as possible. He leaned toward me pushing me back against the wall. Help, we were out of any sight now, oh my god. His body was actually leaning on mine, I could feel the warmth through his jeans. I expected to feel a sharp searing pain somewhere on my body I thought, I don't want to be here. This isn't me, I'm not here right now. I do not want to be here at all, this is NOT HAPPENING, Please...

I couldn't see him and I could only see beard and nose. He paused for what seemed like minutes, and then, with a hard shove he pushed me away. My shoulders, back and head knocked against the brick wall. "Keep a low profile" he said and strutted away. I felt his warm breath and heard the thud of my head internally from hitting the wall. I was stunned and could not move. Not quite sure what had gone on, I expected to feel pain somewhere…. But there was none.

Shaking like a leaf and thanking god, the powers at be any presence that maybe the reason why nothing had happened to me. Thank you, Thank you Thank you…!

I threw up a little from the nerves. I collected myself and commuted home after my encounter with Mr Biker. I cried myself to sleep that night. Sobbing like a little baby, heaving in gasps of air. I questioned everything that evening.

I don't know what our future holds or whether or not the little shop will survive. I don't know if these ladies have any idea how hairy this could get?

I have a career path as a tattoo artists that I chose and am responsible for. I love my job and always dreamed of becoming a tattoo artists, but at this current time, I would change that if given half the chance.

I understand that the biker and gang side of life is part of life's necessary evil… I have watched Son's of Anarchy and was surprised that the 'tattoo shops' were left out as it is common knowledge that they are key bread winners of the underworld. I personally wave the 'baby blue' flag, I mean no disrespect but want to portray a huge message. It's time tattoo shops are about the artists and the customers.

We have now installed full surveillance cameras around the tattoo shop. We did have had a small incident happen and we published the footage on social media and have made it quite clear that we will do this and implicate whomever is trying to hinder our shop. Every time something happens people will be updated. We have made a connection with the local police of our intent and have asked that they look out for us. The footage received over 60K views and we have a small following. I am here to stay and will continue to stand up for my shop. Tattoo Artists are what maketh the Tattoo shop and the customers follow said artists, Tattoo artists should be considered and appreciated. Hopefully more owner artists tattoo shops will emerge, it's a great career, I love every minute of it.

Gratefully I am working with a beautiful team of artists, who share my perspective. My colleagues are like me, career driven artists who are solely about the art and who have values and, like me, strive for a more professional tattoo future.

Wish us luck – "Jaimie Diamond"

I will hold the candle till it burns up my arm
Oh I'll keep takin' punches until their will grows tired
Oh I will stare the sun down until my eyes go blind
Hey, I won't change direction, and I won't change my
mind
How much difference does it make

Indifference by the Band: Pearl Jam – Eddie Vedder

21
I love my job

Although the conditions have been unexpectedly turbulent, working as a tattoo artist is wonderful. The years have educated me to a myriad of alternative understandings. The journey has been demanding at times, but in return, it has been very gratifying. And the sense of accomplishment I have gained when exceeding a customer's expectations cannot be compared. I have illustrated some encounters that I have experienced during my phase as a tattoo artist. My clientele has been delightful and I have loved performing every tattoo.

*Golden Oldie. A lovely little lady I tattooed, and who must have been about 75+ years old. The lady had lost her poodle dog. To commemorate the dog, the lady had acquired a tattoo of her poodle. Sadly, she had not received the best service. She had bought her poodle when her husband passed away, so the whole ordeal was quite distressing to her, as you can imagine... She came to me and asked if I could fix her tattoo and make the tattoo that she received look more like her dog. And add her deceased husband's name in a scroll. It took me a couple of hours, but by the end of the session, the lady had a presentable piece of tattoo art. I was able to work with the tattoo that she had already obtained. Tidying the image to represent the precious poodle and adding her beloved husband's name in a scroll below it. I organised a time and was honoured to be able to turn a negative tattoo experience into a positive one!

"I did not get permission with this image, so here is some of my own art work instead".

*Wedding ring tattoo. An engineer who cannot wear his wedding ring, due to his work commitments. Requested that I design him and his wife, who was very against tattoos, a wedding ring tattoo. This was quite a big deal to them both. As she agreed to have her ring tattooed as well, to match her partner. The style of the wedding ring was to be Celtic, but delicate. I explained that I could. But there were some details that needed to be considered before we went ahead and made the booking. I needed to educate them as to the skin conditions on fingers and how tattooing this area was not so straightforward. You see, on your hands and feet you have a high rate of wear and tear. The skins rejuvenates more often in these areas. This is why the skin in those areas may age more and appear slightly crapey in texture, compared to the skin in the other areas on your body. Tattooing fingers is problematic and may take up to 3 sittings to complete. The application of the tattoo is slightly tricky and there is a very high degree of fall out. Therefore, once healed, the artist would need to re-apply the tattoo again in some areas.

After explaining the details of the area and re-application or multiple performance of the tattoo, the couple decided to go ahead and booked in. The couple came back two more times for the re-application. I met them halfway with the cost, throwing in the last session as a free touch up session. My customers were very happy and I was honoured to work on such a lovely couple.

"I did not get permission with this image, so here is another tattoo piece instead".

*Even Doctors get tattoos. A 70 year old Doctor and his wife had always been intrigued about obtaining a tattoo. His wife had fancied the idea of getting matching tattoos with her hubby, the doctor. After coming in and enquiring about the process, the couple felt comfortable enough to arrange an appointment time. Their design requests were simple, either matching tattoo designs or a tattoo design that could be split into two sections. Making the full image when both designs were placed together. The couple had placed getting a tattoo on their bucket list and I was honoured that they had come to see me.

The doctor wanted a more traditional style tattoo, and I designed a small tattoo for them. They received the same matching tattoos, but on opposite wrists. So, when they held hands, both tattoos would connect.

The doctor was very inquisitive about the sterilisation and the tattoo application procedure. They told me, I had been highly recommended by a friend of theirs. I provided the best tattoo service I could and was tickled to have worked on a doctor!

*50 Year old lady, who has a rocking tattoo sleeve. I had a lady enquire about a cover up tattoo job. I explained that there was a process involved for me to cover up existing tattoo art with another tattoo. I enquired as to what her ultimate end goal would be and got down to designing. The tattoo she had acquired was of an angel, the design was small and over a few years, the detail had blended together. Sadly, the angel looked more like a wizard and, as it was placed on her wrist, people not only notice but would often comment on it as well. She still wanted an angel. I came up with an image that I could use to cover her existing tattoo. The angel image was larger and the design softer. I tried to consider her age and match her overall look. The lady was more than happy with the cover up tattoo, and in short, continued the design into a full sleeve. Yes, the sleeve is from wrist to shoulder and covers the underside of the arm as well.

I did not expect that this customer would become so committed. She is such a sophisticated lady, her tattoo looks amazing. Again, I am humbled to have been chosen to perform your tattoo art work.

*A full back bike engine tattoo. I had a gentleman request that he cover his entire back with his Harley Davidson engine. He enquired about what I thought of the details and specifics, as this was very important to him. He wanted his bike's engine and not just any old Harley Davidson engine. I explained that there was a process for a tattoo piece of that size. That I was happy to take on a tattoo of this type and would need a clear image of the engine. The customer carried out his incremental sessions, until the tattoo was complete. He was punctual and pleasant. He bought me a bottle of wine, when he won a local town tattoo event with his Harley Davison engine back tattoo. He was happy with the service and I was ecstatic to have another happy customer.

*A tattoo to cover over some scars. Scar cover over can be a delicate and sensitive process. I had a young man who bought his partner to me. The young lady had some scarring and was very self-conscious of it. She always wore clothing to hide the scars and was affected by having to do so. They advised me that they had sought my service, as I was a female tattoo artist and would it be possible to cover the scars with a tattoo?

Not only could I cover the area with a tattoo design, but I could also provide a more subtle option as well. The young lady could have the option of a pigment blend. This is where pigment matches the skin colour, and is applied and blended with the scar area. This provides less contrast with the surrounding skin.

They opted for a tattoo design to cover the scarred area. So I created an image to cover the scarred area, making sure it worked in with the contour of her body. So, the cover image flowed nicely and wasn't so stamp-like. We concealed the area with her favourite flowers and some filigree. The young lady came in a few weeks later, wearing a sleeveless dress. Her and her partner gave me a hug. He said it was the first time she had worn this type of clothing out in public. She seemed very self-confident and pleased. I felt on cloud nine to have been able to help.

*Stretch marks can be tricky. Most ladies have some form of stretch marks. Stretch marks form from many different reasons. Body growth from child to adult, weight gain and pregnancy are a few of the main causes. In some people, stretch marks will tend to be a silvery colour and not often hugely visible. However, some people who have a darker skin tone can produce more visibly noticeable stretch marks. A lady came to me wanting to cover her pregnancy stretch marks. She explained that she was very lucky and had re-gained her figure. However, didn't like her stretch marks around her stomach, above the underwear line. Tattooing over stretch marks can be tricky. The skin is stretched in areas and not in others. Therefore, when you perform a single line using tattooing as a method, the inked line is retained tightly in in-tact skin areas, but does not hold its sharp line in the stretched skin areas. This is caused by the damaged elastin content of the skin in the area of the stretch mark. This can leave the stretch mark running very thin and crêpey, in comparison to the intact skin adjacent to the stretch mark. The stretch marked skin retains the pigment just fine. It is the definition we struggle with. Tattoo designs such as script wouldn't be advised as a tattoo in this area. And as a tattoo artist, I needed to consider this when organising the tattoo design. I also considered the positioning and how the overall design would look. I tailored the design symmetrically, so that it would flow with the lady's bikini line on her lower stomach.

I tattooed brightly coloured flowerers and leaves. A design that didn't have harsh edges or outlines. The design covered the area and was the touching finish to the lady's fantastic figure.

"I did not get permission with this image, so here is some of my own art work instead".

*Areola tattoo for a drag queen. Tattoos are not limited to imagery. Some tattoos are cosmetic, and using the tattoo method, are performed to make additional enhancements to one's appearance. The ink is implemented into the skin. Some classifications of this are known as permanent cosmetics and micro-pigmentation. I have assisted a 'lady' with a wondrous nipple creation. The lady was transgender and had undergone significant body modification to achieve her beautiful appearance. I was delighted to have been able to help.

Tattoo Art, Permanent cosmetics and Micropigmentation.

- Permanent cosmetics are achieved using exactly the same process as a tattoo. Ink or pigment is inserted into the skin's dermis by penetration of the skin with surgical needles. Permanent cosmetics use different technology, that provides the same method. Most permanent cosmetics use semi-permanent and organic pigment, which is designed for sensitive skin areas such as the skin surrounding the eyes, eye brows and lips.

Some categories of semi-permanent cosmetics are:

- Eyeliner upper and lower line

- Lid liner, Lash line fill *(this gives you the look of plump and fuller looking lashes at the base of the lash.)* Soft edge, Fade out

- Eyebrows – Shape and shade fill, shape and hair strokes. Recreate using hair stroke techniques known as feather brows.

- Skin Scarring – Camouflage, blend *(colour matching your skin pigment and filling areas of skin that lack pigment or melanin content).*

- Micro Pigmentation – Hair Tattoo

This is where we apply pigment matched to your hair colour and hair follicle dimension. We create a face frame and blend the pigment using small dots. This creates the look of a buzz cut, or close clipper head shave.

We also create density in thinning areas of your scalp. Both men and women are eligible for this service. This application works wonders for keeping up a more youthful appearance. Your service provider will be able to answer any enquires.

- Front Hair line creation. Artistically frame for your face.

- Hair transplant and surgery scars. (We create a pigment blend and hair follicle imagery to eliminate the contrast of your HT scarring).

- Areola re-pigmentation, or creation, this is where pigment is used. The identical way to how a tattoo is performed. A nipple can be artistically created for anyone undergone surgery or other. Additional to this we can also enhance the colour, shape and detail of your existing areola.

I hope this gives you, the customer, more of an insight into the amount of work involved in designing your permanent body art, be it tattoo art, cosmetic or micro-pigmentation.

What is the difference between permanent cosmetics technicians and tattoo artists? Tattoo artists work predominantly with images. However, if your tattoo artist does specialist cosmetic tattoos, be reassured you are likely to be in good hands.

Tattoo artists that cross over and branch into cosmetics as well, generally have an edge over technicians. Tattoo artists tend to be more experienced in skin conditions and what equipment is needed for the desired result. Also, tattoo artists gain years of experience working on many different areas of the skin. Some areas of the skin can retain the pigment differently, and so, depth, needle size and application methods should to be considered. The areas your artist would also consider are:

As the skin ages, elastin levels diminish over time and a slight drop or droop in some areas occur. This is natural in the course of ageing. The body is not symmetrical. And a degree of artistic perspective is needed. This ensures the best application is performed. As tattoo artists, we often apply images that need to work with the body's flow. Symmetrical images applied on imbalanced bodies can be challenging. Objectionable perspectives and knowledge are crucial, when working in permanency of any kind.

I love my job

Jaimie Diamond's informative guide to getting a tattoo

The tattoo industry has grown with popularity, and the demand has seen an increase in service providers or contracting artists. Some artists have taken it upon themselves to perform the tattoo service from their home or garage, rather than working in an apparently 'professional' environment, such as a tattoo shop. These home working artists are known as back yard artists. These artists generally purchase cheaper products, that are not supplied by registered tattoo and piercing suppliers. They also do not have to comply with any council, state and service regulations. Thus, they are able to considerably discount the service cost. Financially persuaded customers think that they are getting a good or the same level of service or performance of their tattoo. But at a cheaper rate as explained. In fact, they are not!

In my dream world here, fellow artists are predominantly shop owners. The services and artistic qualities are of the forefront of the provided services. And the biker gangs are out of the picture. Here is how I see that services could be made more beneficial for both the customers and the contracting artists

A non-thug like greeting – a "Hello" or "How are you today?". Walking into a tattoo shop can be slightly unnerving, so a nice greeting from the front of house staff is always greatly received.

I always consider the possibility of a potential customer and want to make anyone who comes into the shop feel warm and invited. Artists are to provide a service, it is a luxury to be working on the customers. It is not a luxury for the

customer to be 'grunted at' because it isn't cool. Make the potential customer feel comfortable, help with their enquiry and book them in for a tattoo…

As a customer, if you have a design request, we can offer you advice and information on how to go about obtaining the design. It is our job to educate you on the size, placement, session sitting, and cost.

Please note that, sometimes, when you enquire about a tattoo and the cost of the design, we will not be sure until the design has been modified and sized. Detail, size, comprehensive art styles and colour all play a factor. Placing an accurate cost on the design can be difficult, but we should be able to provide a minimum and maximum cost quotation.

If you are getting a tattoo custom drawn for you and the shop wants to book you in, there should be an acceptable draw up time frame for example 3 – 14 days. Your artist should be in contact with you within that time frame to go over the concept he or she has designed. There is normally a cost that is associated with that design process. Please consider that work on your design takes a fair bit of time. We will generally charge a deposit fee to ensure that you are serious about acquiring your tattoo; And so that the artist doesn't spend time illustrating your tattoo design for nothing…

Deposits are mandatory in most tattoo shops. So, expect to pay a deposit when you go to book in your for tattoo. It's best to generally bring cash at this stage. But, who knows maybe in the future you will be able to pay with your banking card.... You can at my shop.

Pricing your tattoo: Generally the tattoo shop will have a set hourly rate and a minimum charge. Some of the downfalls associated with tattoo shops is that they host a myriad of skill levels and what you receive from one person may take another artist twice as long. I urge you, as a consumer, to enquire as to how long the artist has been tattooing for? I have worked in shops that have charged out 'slow' artists using an hourly rate. Nine times out of ten, these shops do not care about their tattoo output and are solely focussed on tattoo time and monetary amount. Most good tattoo shops have an idea of the time it may take to perform a certain sized tattoo. If one artist quotes you, you do not have to take that as gospel. Feel free to enquire about the cost from another artist. Too many people are getting ripped off and having poor experiences, so by assuming some of the responsibility, hopefully, we can make the journey more pleasing. I, myself, use a business card. I can complete the surface area of that card in one hour, twice that would equal two hours, and so on.

Designing your master piece: You should be able to talk openly with your artist or the shop front of house staff. The artist should also have an up to date portfolio, demonstrating their own performed tattoo art for you to view. Do not be afraid to be critical. You have probably been online and seen some tattoos or perhaps watched some of the reality T.V shows about tattoos. And you are aware that you can have a really nice piece of artwork. If the artists do not demonstrate that standard or level then, feel free to ask for another artist or check out another shop.

Communication is crucial, and if you cannot talk to your artist or the front of house person in confidence about your design, then leave and find a better tattoo shop. Do not be badgered or forced into getting your tattoo. There are many shops that still make you feel intimidated in order to get you booked in. This is disgusting in this day and age and should not be entertained.

Booking and management: Depending on your tattoo and the tattoo shop's workload, you may be booked in, or asked to attend another day. You should be given a receipt for your deposit and a time that suits you will be organised. You should also be given advice, especially if it is your first tattoo.

1. Make sure you have eaten that day, a little more than two bites of toast please, ladies. As your artist, we want you to have a beautiful piece of art work. Part of achieving that is having the customer complete the session easily. Your body's energy levels aid that ease. Food is advised.

2. Please do not come in after drinking more than two standard drinks the night before. This can affect how you skin retains the pigment and how you cope with the session.

3. For some reason, if you cannot make it, please call and re-schedule. Some shops will keep your deposit, if you have not notified them of the cancellation 24 hours prior to your scheduled time. There is a fair amount of preparation in setting up for a customer, and most of the time, your artist will have worked on your design prior to your appointment. It is common courtesy to re-schedule and let the shop know, if you cannot make your appointment ahead of time.

Tattoo time: When you arrive, please be on time. If you are late, you may get rebooked due to booking schedules. If you are early, please be patient; have a look at the magazines in the waiting area and relax. Your artist should be running on time. We understand that you are slightly nervous and we will do the best to make you feel at ease. Most artists will explain the process and take you through the steps. The experience, although slightly uncomfortable, should be a good one.

Sitting through your tattoo: Please make sure that you sit still during your tattoo. And although you may be a little nervous or excited, you should be in good hands. Hopefully, you have taken the advice and had some breakfast or lunch that day. Relax and breathe. Getting a tattoo should be good experience.

In a tattoo shop you will be presented with the sterilised equipment for your tattoo or piecing. You should view the sterilised or new equipment prior to signing your consent form. You are entitled to see the instruments being used. They should be opened in front of you. Disposable equipment will have an expiry date, batch number and will be sealed in an unhampered package. Re-usable stainless steel equipment should be in a sealed autoclave bag. This bag should be opened in front of you also. The autoclave bag or pouch, that contains the equipment, will have a process indicator on the back. This indicator will change colour when adequate gas or steam sterilisation has occurred. You should ask to view this and even compare the indicator colour change to an unsterilised bag. Again, feel free to ask.

The responsibility lies with the YOU the customer. And no matter how 'clean' the back yard performer may claim to be, it is still a large risk to take. Especially when the difference in cost may only be between $50 – $100 dollars...Cheep inks purchased from budget unregistered suppliers have been found to not have undergone adequate trials and testing. Your safety may be compromised with cheap tattoo pigment that has been obtained from other unregistered sources. Some of the inks have been found to have high carbon and bacteria contents, even cancer causing bacteria...Some inks have been recalled. Unlicensed suppliers use selling platforms to move the tattoo ink, relabelling them if necessary.

Under age customers: Most under 18 year olds will need parent consent to acquire a tattoo. Please be mindful that tattoos are popular, but are not hugely acceptable in the work place. The design, size and placement may hinder future work options. Your artist may ask you to take this into consideration.

Tattoo suppliers generally only supply tattoo and piercing equipment and products to registered shops and register red artists. If the country or state of the artist does not have regulations for the artists to be licensed, then the tattoo house or shop would need to provide evidence that the inks and equipment used are, in fact, adequate.

The tattoo inks have the following details: Brand name and product colour description. The ingredients will be clearly visible on the label. The label will also contain a LOT, batch, and date of produce. Expiry dates and manufacturer details will also be printed.

Seriously, no drinks, beforehand. You also would have been advised of this when you made your booking. And in the consent form or disclaimer, there may be a question related to blood thinning drugs or alcohol in relation to your consumption. The reason for this; If you have consumed alcohol and or any blood thinning agents, we cannot ensure the quality of your tattoo.

Once your tattoo has been finished, you will be asked to have a look and make sure you're happy. Also, if there are any areas you may want to add then let your artist know. You should be given an after care advice form, explaining how to look after your newly performed tattoo.

Some key steps are:

Treat your tattoo like a wounded knee or burn, keep it clean. Apply your aftercare sparingly, rubbing the cream in until it is completely absorbed. If you attend the gym and work on the public apparatus, please consider the high bacteria content on those areas and cover your tattoo during your work out. Clean it directly after. Your tattoo should flake and coloured skin flakes should fall off. This takes around 3-7 days, depending on how your skin heals. There maybe a little scabbing but nothing too dramatic should occur. The tattoo will continue to flake and be shiny for around 5 weeks. After that, you will notice change. Some people describe the black ink changing to a 'blue' colour. This is where the skin has accepted the pigment. The colour hasn't changed, it has just adopted the melanin content (skin colour tone) of your skin. If there are any concerns, drop your artist a line or message. We generally care about our artwork and hope that if you do decide to get another tattoo in the future, you will come back to see us.

If you find that there are small patches of colour, or that some of the outline has come out of the tattoo with the skin flake, be sure to let your artist know and organise a touch up sitting with them. This touch up session shouldn't cost anything, and if it does, it will normally be a minimal charge. Some tattoo shops have a timeframe of about five to six weeks after the tattoo has been performed that you may need to comply with. This session is known as a touch up session and you may be asked to come in during that time period, not after. If you forget about having your tattoo touched up, please be aware that if you go back four months or later down the track, you may be charged additionally. It is very hard to determine how a tattoo is looked after, and we artists do not get to go home with you to make sure you are looking after 'our' but your artwork, your new tattoo. How you look after your tattoo while it heals is important, and can impact your overall end result.

And please understand that no one other than you is responsible for the choice of design, who performs your tattoo and how it is looked after during the healing process…I hope you enjoy your tattoo experience!

Quotations and Aspirations

"In life, people tend to wait for good things to come to them. And by waiting, they miss out. Usually, what you wish for doesn't fall in your lap; it falls somewhere nearby, and you have to recognise it, stand up, and put in the time and work it takes to get to it. This isn't because the universe is cruel. It's because the universe is smart. It has its own cat-string theory and knows we don't appreciate things that fall into our laps."

— Neil Strauss, *The Game: Penetrating the Secret Society of Pickup Artists*

"When one with honeyed words but evil mind persuades the mob, great woes befall the state."

— Euripides, Orestes

"It is your work in life that is the ultimate seduction."

— Picasso

Research and reference

- **Hepatitis C Virus and its transmission**

Hepatitis C is a virus which can cause damage to the liver. Hepatitis C virus is transmitted by transfer of blood, most commonly through drug users sharing needles. It was also transmitted through blood transfusions or blood products prior to screening of donated blood for hepatitis C. **Non-sterile tattooing or body piercing equipment also possess a risk of hepatitis C transmission**. The virus may also be transmitted from mother to child at birth (7%). However, it is much less infectious than hepatitis B and does not spread as readily. The risk of sexual transmission (5%) appears to be very low, provided no blood-to-blood contact occurs.

What happens to those infected?

Some people lose the virus, approximately 20% in the 1st year of infection, but in many cases, they will become chronically infected with the virus. These people have been infected with hepatitis C, and instead of getting rid of it, "carry" it in their liver for many years. They often experience fatigue and other problems such as joint pain and skin irritations. In the long-term, they are at risk from progressive liver damage.

- **Independent contractor**

From Wikipedia, the free encyclopedia

An **independent contractor** is a natural person, business, or corporation that provides goods or services to another entity under terms specified in a contract or within a verbal agreement. Unlike an employee, an independent contractor does not work regularly for an employer, but works as and when required, during which time he or she may be subject to law of agency. Independent contractors are usually paid on a freelance basis. Contractors often work through a limited company or franchise, which they themselves own, or may work through an umbrella company.

In the United States, any company or organisation engaged in a trade or business that pays more than $600 to an independent contractor in one year is required to report this to the Internal Revenue Service (IRS), as well as to the contractor. This form is merely a report of the money paid; independent contractors **do not have income taxes withheld from their pay as regular employees do.**

- **ACT**

Any business, charity, demonstration or service that carries out a *skin penetration procedure* or an *infection risk procedure* is regulated under Part III of the *ACT Public Health Act 1997* and must comply with the standards set in an applicable Code of Practice. A *skin penetration procedure* is any process that involves the piercing, cutting, puncturing or tearing of a living human body. An *infection risk procedure* is any process that involves the administration of make up, or other like substances on human skin or mucus membrane, or any process that involves the insertion of instruments, equipment, foreign objects, substances or other matter inside a human body for cosmetic or therapeutic purposes.

Skin penetration procedures have been declared licensable public health risk activities under the *Public Health Act 1997* and businesses that carry out skin penetration procedures, such as tattooing and body piercing are required to hold a Public Health Risk Activity (Infection Control) Business Licence. Businesses whose skin penetration activities are limited to *infection risk.*

The Code and Guidelines cover many infection control practices including:

- provision of written "after care" advice;
- use of single use and reusable equipment;
- premises construction;
- handling and disposal of sharps and clinical wastes;
- personal protective equipment and immunisation;
- aseptic technique and skin disinfectants;
- environmental cleaning, including dealing with blood and body substance spills; and
- reprocessing of appliances.

Section 388 ACT *Children and Young People Act 1999*

In New South Wales, the following legislation relates to Infection Control in the Body Art

Industry:

- Section 51 of the *Public Health Act 1991*;

- Public Health (Skin Penetration) Regulation 2000; and

- Section 28 of the *Children (Care and Protection) Act 1998*.

A skin penetration procedure is defined to mean acupuncture, tattooing, ear piercing, hair removal, any other procedure (whether medical or not) that involves skin penetration, and any other procedure prescribed by the regulations (colonic lavage is prescribed as a skin penetration procedure).

Procedures carried out in the practice of a registered medical practitioner, dentist, chiropractor, osteopath, dental technician, nurse, optical dispenser, optometrist, and a psychologist are exempt. Similarly, procedures carried out by a person acting under the direction or supervision of such a professional as part of that professional's practice is exempt. (These professions are covered by separate infection control guidelines).

The Regulation provides for basic standards in relation to premises where skin penetration procedures are conducted and the articles and equipment (including protective equipment) used in such procedures.

A person carrying out skin penetration must notify the local authority of the address of the premises. This requirement also extends to mobile operators. Local authorities are required to maintain a register of premises in their area at which skin penetration procedures are carried out.

The Regulation provides for the making of the Guidelines on Skin Penetration and blood cholesterol testing or blood screening and anything done in compliance with those guidelines is a defence for a prosecution for an offence. The Guidelines set out basic infection control requirements consistent with the Regulation. Whilst not a statutory requirement, the public health unit has also developed a Code of Best Practice, which sets out recommended (more extensive) standards with respect to matters such as disinfection, waste disposal, sterilisation and cleaning.

The *Children (Care and Protection) Act 1998* provides that it is an offence to tattoo a person under the age of 18 years, without first obtaining the written consent of a parent of the child to tattoo the child in that manner and on that part of the child's body.

NEW ZEALAND

There is no dedicated legislation specifically related to the Body Art industry in New Zealand. Tattooing and body piercing is currently not subject to any specific legislative controls in New Zealand.

These practices are subject to generic consumer safety legislation (administered by the Ministry of Consumer Affairs) and the *Health and Safety in Employment Act 1992* (for the body artistes themselves). The nuisance provisions of the *Health Act 1956* (any conditions which are "offensive or likely to be injurious to health") could apply, and these are enforced by local government.

Additionally, any one of 74 city or district councils could also make local by-laws that might also apply.

In order to protect public health safety in relation to tattooing and body piercing, the Ministry of Health in 1998 produced Guidelines for the Safe Piercing of Skin. The guidelines explain:

- how to minimise the risk of transmitting blood borne and other infections by the use of standard precautions during skin piercing procedures;

- how to ensure appliances are clean and sterile before being used for skin piercing;

- how to minimise the risk of transmitting micro-organisms between the operator, the appliances used and other clients; and

- how to further promote a safe work environment for workers performing skin piercing operations.

Operators, who offer body piercing and tattooing services to promote minimum standards with respect to infection control in this industry, use these guidelines. Although there is expectation that operators will use the guidelines, there is no legislative requirement for this to occur.

The *Health Act* is currently the subject of a major review process (expected to be replaced by a new *Public Health Act* in a couple of years), and it is possible that in future regulations could be developed in relation to tattooing and body piercing.

NORTHERN TERRITORY

The Northern Territory has no legislation specific to infection control in the Body Art industry. However, it has Standards for Commercial Skin Penetration, Hairdressing and Beauty and Natural Therapy. If an operator were in breach of those Standards, environmental health officers would be able to use the provisions of the Public Health (General Sanitation etc) Regulations under the *Public Health Act* to prevent a risk to health.

The *Public Health Act* is under review. The proposal in relation to public health risk activities is that the Minister will prescribe certain high-risk activities by notice in the Gazette. It is expected that body piercing will be a prescribed activity. Any activities so prescribed will have to be registered and persons carrying out the activity will have to adhere to any Code of Practice or conditions attached to the registration. Failure to do so will be an offence and could also result in cancellation of the licence.

QUEENSLAND

In Queensland, the following legislation relates to Infection Control in the Body Art Industry:

- Health Regulation 1996 – Part 15 – Skin Penetration.

The legislation sets out infection control requirements for skin penetration operators such as tattooists and body piercers. It applies to acupuncture and electrolysis and any other process where the skin is penetrated. There are exemptions for practitioners such as medical practitioners, dentists. There is no guideline, which compliments this legislation.

Under the current legislation, local governments throughout Queensland enforce Part 15 and can charge an annual $200 premise registration fee to cover costs of enforcement and administration. It is a requirement that business operators register their premises with the local government.

The legislation is currently under review, under the National Competition Policy requirements. A consultant was engaged to prepare a Risk Report and Public Benefit Test report. These documents formed the basis of a regulatory model for the hairdressing, beauty therapy, tattooing and body piercing industries in relation to infection control. New legislation with a complimentary guideline covering these practices is currently under development. A Regulatory Impact Statement is required, but has not been prepared to date. It is expected that the new legislation will be in place in July 2002.

Of particular note is that the Risk Report identified through a risk profile (higher risk, moderate risk, lower risk) that higher risk operators such as tattooists and body piercers should successfully complete a basic training course in infection control and this requirement is included in draft legislation. It will be a breach of legislation if these operators are found practising without a statement stating they have successfully completed such a training course.

The higher risk business proprietor will be required to obtain a business licence from the local government in which their business is located. Building requirements for higher risk practices will be in place in the Building Code of Australia. Local governments will be able to charge a fee for one routine inspection per year only. If an inspection on complaint results in the service of a remedial notice, an inspection fee may be charged to determine compliance with the notice. Local governments will have the power to suspend or cancel business licences.

SOUTH AUSTRALIA

In South Australia, the following legislation relates to Body Art industry:

- *Summary Offences Act 1953*; and

- *Public and Environmental Health Act 1987*.

Age of Consent – It is an offence to tattoo a minor (under 18) under S21A of *the Summary Offences Act 1953.* A Private Member's Bill is currently before Parliament to extend that to cover other body piercing of children.

Sections 15 & 17 of the *Public and Environmental Health Act 1987* give local councils powers to remedy insanitary conditions or activities giving rise to a risk to health. Guidelines have been issued to assist councils and persons engaging in skin penetration activities in proper infection control procedures. They could form the basis for a notice under those sections if an operator in the industry has inadequate procedures.

SA Health Commission Guidelines on the Safe and Hygienic Practice of Skin Penetration were issued in November 1995. They cover:

- aseptic or "non-touch" procedures;
- cleaning disinfection & sterilisation of equipment;
- disinfectants;
- hand washing and personal hygiene;
- skin preparation;
- needle stick injuries and cleaning of wounds;
- general hygiene;
- waste disposal;
- disposal of sharps; and
- storage & safe handling of chemicals.

A review of the guidelines has just commenced involving industry, local council

WESTERN AUSTRALIA

In Western Australia, the following legislation relates to Body Art Industry:

- *Health (Skin Penetration Procedure) Regulations 1998* (the Regulations); and

- Section 138A of the *Child Welfare Act* 1947.

The Regulations were brought into operation on 1 June 1998 and were made under section 343A as read with section 249(10) of the *Health Act 1911*.

The Regulations adopt the "Code of Practice for Skin Penetration Procedures (Western Australia Department of Health)" (the Code) which was developed and published by the Executive Director, Public Health under section 344A(2) of the Act. There is no Regulation Impact Statement requirement in Western Australia.

The Regulations were made to assist in preventing the spread of blood-borne infectious diseases such as Human Immunodeficiency Virus (HIV) infection and Hepatitis B and C during the course of skin penetration procedures as undertaken in the body piercing; tattooing; acupuncture and beauty therapy industries.

The Regulations do not have application to skin penetration procedures carried out by -

- medical practitioners and dentists and persons acting under their direction and supervision;
- podiatrists; and
- nurses.

The Regulations also required owners of establishments, where skin penetration procedures are or are intended to be carried out, to notify the relevant local government of the name and address of the establishment. Such notice is required to enable local governments to institute appropriate public health surveillance mechanisms to ensure that the Regulations are being complied with.

The Regulations may need some slight change, following a consultation process that is concluding shortly.

The Code sets out the minimum standards of infection control that must be complied with by anyone who performs a skin penetration procedure, which includes any procedure that punctures, cuts or tears the skin or mucous membrane. It is procedure based and provides specific direction to the acupuncture, beauty therapy, body piercing and tattooing industries.

The Code has the general acceptance of industry and consumers and is working well. The Department of Consumer and Employment Protection have also developed a "Code of Practice on the Management of HIV/AIDs and Hepatitis at Workplaces". This Code covers 'Body Art' matters and is tied into the WA *Occupational Safety and Health Act 1984* through the Occupational Safety and Health Regulations 1996.

CONCLUSION

As evidenced by the snapshot of legislation in each jurisdiction provided in this Review, although **there is wide variation the Body Art industry, it** is nevertheless regulated to some extent in all jurisdictions. While some jurisdictions have specific legislation, others manage the industry through Standards and Codes of Practice and some have both. In order to obtain a complete picture of the situation with regard to the Body Art industry, a detailed study would be required to examine related issues such as age of consent (reflected in South Australia) and training of **personnel undertaking employment in the industry**. It would also be useful to examine enforcement/implementation mechanisms for the legislation, standards and codes of practice, in order to understand the successes and failures of the existing systems.

Glossary

A hit – An action toward another. It can be a drive by shooting, or an up closed walk in and shoot, stab or beat the person intended for the 'hit'. Either situation can have dire consequence for people, families and loved ones.

Old school – In slang, "**old school**" or "old skool" can refer to anything that is from an earlier era or anything that may be considered "old-fashioned". The term is commonly used to suggest a high regard for something that has been shown to have lasting value or quality.

New School – **New school** is a tattooing style originating as early as the 1970s and influenced by some features of old school tattooing in the United States. The style is often characterized by the use of heavy outlines, vivid colours, and exaggerated depictions of the subject. New school also represents a transition towards openness in the sharing of techniques in tattooing.

Territory – *States and territories of Australia, administrative subdivisions of Australia

*Territoriality (nonverbal communication), how people use space to communicate ownership/occupancy of areas and possessions

Biker – * a rider of a bicycle

* a rider of a motorcycle, i.e., one who participates in motorcycling

* a member of an outlaw motorcycle club

Gang – A **gang** is a group of recurrently associating individuals or close friends or family with identifiable leadership and internal organization, identifying with or claiming control over territory in a community, and engaging either individually or collectively in violent or illegal behaviour.[2] Some criminal gang members are "jumped in" or have to prove their loyalty by committing acts such as theft or violence. Although gangs exist internationally, there is a greater level of study and knowledgeable information of gangs specifically in the United States. A member of a gang may be called a gangster or a thug.

Contractor – Subcontractor, an individual or business that signs a contract to perform part or all of the obligations of another's contract.

Tattoo artist – A **tattoo artist** (also **tattooer** or **tattooist**) is an individual who applies permanent decorative tattoos, often in an established business called a "tattoo shop," "tattoo studio" or '"tattoo parlour." Tattoo artists usually learn their craft via an apprenticeship under a trained and experienced mentor.

Back Yard Tattooist / Scratchers – People who tattoo without proper training in the art of tattooing are commonly known as 'scratchers'. Scratchers often operate from home, but may also operate from an unlicensed studio, making it difficult for customers to identify whether the artist is legitimate or not. In addition, scratchers may offer reduced rates in order to attract customers away from professional tattoo shops. In the USA, practicing without a license is a criminal offence in many states.[5]

The practice of tattooing without proper training also carries serious health risks. Studies have shown that there is a significant risk of contracting Hepatitis C when tattoos are carried out using cheap, unsterilised tattooing equipment.

These risks are found to be higher on unregulated premises.[6]

In the UK, Plymouth City Council launched a campaign in 2014 to crack down on 'scratchers' operating within the city "in an attempt to reduce infection and injury through better awareness".

Extortion − **Extortion** (also called **shakedown, outwrestling**, and **exaction**) is a criminal offense of obtaining money, property, or services from a person, entity, or institution, through coercion. It is sometimes euphemistically referred to as a "protection racket" since the racketeers often phrase their demands as payment for "protection" from (real or hypothetical) threats from unspecified other parties. Extortion is commonly practiced by organized crime groups. The actual obtainment of money or property is not required to commit the offense. Making a threat of violence which refers to a requirement of a payment of money or property to halt future violence is sufficient to commit the offense. Exaction refers not only to extortion or the unlawful demanding and obtaining of something through force,[1] but additionally, in its formal definition, means the infliction of something such as pain and suffering or making somebody endure something unpleasant.[2]

Extortion is distinguished from robbery. In robbery, whether armed or not, the offender takes property from the victim by the immediate use of force or fear that force will be immediately used (as in the classic line, "Your money or your life.") Extortion, which is not limited to the taking of property, involves the verbal or written *instillation* of fear that something will happen to the victim if they do not comply with the extortionist's will. Another key distinction is that extortion always involves a verbal or written threat, whereas robbery does not. In United States federal law, extortion can be committed with or without the use of force and with or without the use of a weapon.

In blackmail, which always involves extortion, the extortionist threatens to reveal information about a victim or their family members that is potentially embarrassing, socially damaging, or incriminating unless a demand for money, property, or services is met.

The term *extortion* is often used metaphorically to refer to usury or to price-gouging, though neither is legally considered extortion. It is also often used loosely to refer to everyday situations where one person feels indebted against their will, to another, in order to receive an essential service or avoid legal consequences.

Neither extortion nor blackmail requires a threat of a criminal act, such as violence, merely a threat used to elicit actions, money, or property from the object of the extortion.

Such threats include the filing of reports (true or not) of criminal behaviour to the police, revelation of damaging facts (such as pictures of the object of the extortion in a compromising position), etc.

Stand-over – using intimidation or threat of force to coerce others into submission or compliance. e.g. "standover tactics" or "standover man".

Tattoo flash – A **tattoo flash** is a stereotypical[1] tattoo design printed or drawn on paper or cardboard, and may be regarded as a species of industrial design. It is typically displayed on the walls of tattoo parlours and in binders to give walk-in customers ideas for tattoos. Most traditional tattoo flash was designed for rapid tattooing and used in "street shops" – tattoo shops that handle a large volume of generic tattoos for walk-in customers.[2]

Flash is either drawn by the individual tattooer for display and used in their own studio, or traded and sold among other tattooers. Hand-drawn, local tattoo flash was largely replaced by professional "flash artists" who produced prints of copyrighted flash and sold them at conventions or through the Internet. By 2000, most tattoo studios have become custom shops with the flash serving as more of a reference for ideas. Most designs are created by the tattoo artist from an idea brought in by the customer. There is no standard size for tattoo flash, but it is most commonly found on 11x14 inch prints in North America, and at A3 paper size in Europe. Tattoo flash may or may not come with an outline, also known as a line drawing. This outline is typically printed on a separate sheet. This is convenient for the tattoo artist, who would otherwise have to draw the line work for themselves.

Tattoo Artist – A Tattoo artist traditionally earns the title by completing an apprenticeship under strict guidelines from an experienced senior tattoo artist. Apprentices are generally expected to be excellent at drawing, with an ability to excel at customizing design ideas and genres, as well as various other styles of art in general.[1]

A tattoo apprenticeship traditionally lasts two years. For the first six months to a year, the apprentice is not allowed to tattoo but is trained in sanitation and proper safety techniques. The apprentice will be expected to clean and maintain the shop, as well as watch and continue to grow as an artist. This first year most apprentices quit and never achieve full completion. The cost of apprenticing can range from free labour around the shop to tens of thousands of dollars.

Artwork

Tattoo artists can create original tattoo designs for their customers. Tattooists may use flash (pre-drawn, stock images that can be traced onto the skin) or variations of known designs.

Tools

Some of the tools of the trade have greatly evolved while some have stayed the same, such as the tattoo machine. In itself, the traditional machine has not changed from its original design and/or concept. With the rise of new machine designs, however, both air- and electric-powered tools such as the rotary and pneumatic tattoo machine have made their way into the industry. A practitioner may also use many different needle sets, such as round liner needles, round shader needles, flat shaders, and magnum (mag) needles. The amount of needles attached to the needle bar change, as well. For instance, large magnum needle groups range from 15 to 55 needles on one bar. There are cheap needle alternatives that have poor hardness and therefore blunt quickly. A practitioner must have the basic tools to provide a tattoo. All other items at the artist's disposal are as different as each tattoo. Basic tools include the tattoo machine, power supply, clip cord, foot pedal, grip, tips, grip stem, needles, and tattoo ink. In the UK equipment must only be sold to registered studios who are provided a certificate by their local environmental health department.[2]

Permanent cosmetics – **Permanent makeup** is a cosmetic technique which employs tattoos (permanent pigmentation of the dermis) as a means of producing designs that resemble makeup, such as eyelining and other permanent enhancing colors to the skin of the face, lips, and eyelids. It is also used to produce artificial eyebrows, particularly in people who have lost them as a consequence of old age, disease, such as alopecia totalis, chemotherapy, or a genetic disturbance, and to disguise scars and white spots in the skin such as in vitiligo. It is also used to restore or enhance the breast's areola, such as after breast surgery.

Most commonly called **permanent cosmetics**, other names include **dermapigmentation**, **micropigmentation**, and **cosmetic tattooing**,[1] the latter being most appropriate since permanent makeup is, in fact, tattooing. In the United States and under similar arrangements in some other countries, the colourant additives used in permanent makeup pigments are subject to pre-market approval as cosmetics and or colour additives under the Federal Food, Drug, and Cosmetic Act. However because of other competing public health priorities and a previous lack of evidence of safety problems specifically associated with these pigments, FDA traditionally has not exercised regulatory authority for colour additives on the pigments used in tattoo inks

Micro-pigmentation – Permanent makeup is a cosmetic technique which employs tattoos (permanent pigmentation of the dermis) as a means of producing designs that resemble makeup, such as eyelining and other permanent enhancing colors to the skin of the face, lips, and eyelids. It is also used to produce artificial eyebrows, particularly in people who have lost them as a consequence of old age, disease, such as alopecia totalis, chemotherapy, or a genetic disturbance, and to disguise scars and white spots in the skin such as in vitiligo. It is also used to restore or enhance the breast's areola, such as after breast surgery.

Most commonly called **permanent cosmetics**, other names include **dermapigmentation**, **micropigmentation**, and **cosmetic tattooing**,[1] the latter being most appropriate since permanent makeup is, in fact, tattooing. In the United States and under similar arrangements in some other countries, the colourant additives used in permanent makeup pigments are subject to pre-market approval as cosmetics and or colour additives under the Federal Food, Drug, and Cosmetic Act. However because of other competing public health priorities and a previous lack of evidence of safety problems specifically associated with these pigments, FDA traditionally has not exercised regulatory authority for colour additives on the pigments used in tattoo inks

Pigment – A **pigment** is a material that changes the colour of reflected or transmitted light as the result of wavelength-selective absorption. This physical process differs from fluorescence, phosphorescence, and other forms of luminescence, in which a material emits light.

Many materials selectively absorb certain wavelengths of light. Materials that humans have chosen and developed for use as pigments usually have special properties that make them ideal for colouring other materials. A pigment must have a high tinting strength relative to the materials it colors. It must be stable in solid form at ambient temperatures.

For industrial applications, as well as in the arts, permanence and stability are desirable properties. Pigments that are not permanent are called fugitive. Fugitive pigments fade over time, or with exposure to light, while some eventually blacken.

Pigments are used for colouring paint, ink, plastic, fabric, cosmetics, food and other materials. Most pigments used in manufacturing and the visual arts are dry colorants, usually ground into a fine powder. This powder is added to a binder (or vehicle), a relatively neutral or colourless material that suspends the pigment and gives the paint its adhesion.

A distinction is usually made between a pigment, which is insoluble in its vehicle (resulting in a suspension), and a dye, which either is itself a liquid or is soluble in its vehicle (resulting in a solution). A colorant can act as either a pigment or a dye depending on the vehicle involved. In some cases, a pigment can be manufactured from a dye by precipitating a soluble dye with a metallic salt. The resulting pigment is called a lake pigment. The term biological pigment is used for all coloured substances independent of their solubility.

In 2006, around 7.4 million tons of inorganic, organic and special pigments were marketed worldwide. Asia has the highest rate on a quantity basis followed by Europe and North America. By 2020, revenues will have risen to approx. US$34.2 billion[1] The global demand on pigments was roughly US$ 20.5 billion in 2009, around 1.5-2% up from the previous year. It is predicted to increase in a stable growth rate in the coming years. The worldwide sales are said to increase up to US$ 24.5 billion in 2015, and reach US$ 27.5 billion in 2018

Technician – Experienced technicians in a specific tool domain typically have intermediate understanding of theory and expert proficiency in technique. As such, technicians are generally better versed in technique compared to average laymen and even general professionals in that field of technology. For example, although audio technicians are not as learned in acoustics as acoustical engineers, they are more proficient in operating sound equipment, and they will likely know more about acoustics than other studio staff such as performers.

Technicians may be classified as either highly skilled workers or at times semi-skilled workers, and may be part of a larger (production) process. They may be found working in a variety of fields, and they usually have a job title with the designation 'technician' following the particular category of work. Thus a 'stage technician' is a worker who provides technical support for putting on a play, while a 'medical technician' is an employee who provides technical support in the medical industry or to the medical profession. An engineering technician in the UK is a highly skilled, highly educated occupation requiring 5–8 years post high school training in a formal apprenticeship and college of further education.

Service provider – A **service provider** (**SP**) is a company that provides organizations with consulting, legal, real estate, education, communications, storage, processing, and many other services. Although the term *service provider* can refer to organizational sub-units, it is more generally used to refer to third party or outsourced suppliers, including telecommunications service providers (TSPs), application service providers (ASPs), storage service providers (SSPs), and Internet service providers(ISPs).[citation needed]

IT professionals sometimes differentiate between service providers by categorizing them as type I, II, or III.[1] The three service types are recognized by the IT industry although specifically defined by ITIL and the US Telecommunications Act of 1996

- Type I: internal service provider
- Type II: shared service provider
- Type III: external service provider

Type III SPs provide IT services to external customers and subsequently can be referred to as external service providers (ESPs)[2] which range from a full IT organization/service outsource via managed services or MSPs (managed service providers) to limited product feature delivery via ASPs (application service providers).

House, shop, studio, parlour or premise – The properly equipped tattoo studio will use biohazard containers for objects that have come into contact with blood or bodily fluids, sharps containers for old needles, and an autoclave for sterilizing tools. Certain jurisdictions also require studios by law to have a sink in the work area supplied with both hot and cold water.

Proper hygiene requires a body modification artist to wash his or her hands before starting to prepare a client for the stencil, between clients, after a tattoo has been completed, and at any other time where cross contamination can occur. The use of single use disposable gloves is also mandatory. In some countries and U.S. states it is illegal to tattoo a minor even with parental consent, and it is usually not allowed to tattoo impaired persons (e.g. someone intoxicated or under the influence of drugs), people with contraindicated skin conditions, those who are pregnant or nursing, or those incapable of consent due to mental incapacity. Before the tattooing begins the client is asked to approve the position of the applied stencil. After approval is given the artist will open new, sterile needle packages in front of the client, and always use new, sterile or sterile disposable instruments and supplies, and fresh ink for each session (loaded into disposable ink caps which are discarded after each client). Also, all areas which may be touched with contaminated gloves will be wrapped in clear plastic to prevent cross-contamination. Equipment that cannot be autoclaved (such as countertops, machines, and furniture) will be cleaned with a low level disinfectant and then wiped with an approved high level disinfectant.

The local health department can/will do a hands on inspection of tattoo studios every 4 months in the state of Tennessee. The venue will be graded based on the areas being inspected. If the studio passes an inspection, the health department will sign off on a passing scorecard and the studio will be required to show their score publicly. If the studio fails an inspection, they will be given the opportunity to correct the mistakes (if minor) or be fined (major health risks) and can also be placed out of business on the spot.

Also, the possession of a working autoclave is mandatory in most states. An autoclave is a medical sterilization device used to sterilize stainless steel. The autoclave itself will be inspected by the health department and required to submit weekly spore tests. However if these jurisdictions are up to date, they will not require an autoclave if the practitioners are using 100% disposable tubes and grips which are made of plastic and some grips are made of rubber. These come pre-sterilized for one time use.

Membership in professional organizations, or certificates of appreciation/achievement, generally helps artists to be aware of the latest trends. However, many of the most notable tattooists do not belong to any association. While specific requirements to become a tattooist vary between jurisdictions, many mandate only formal training in blood-borne pathogens, and cross contamination. The local department of health regulates tattoo studios in many jurisdictions.

For example, according to the health departments in Oregon and Hawaii, tattoo artists in these states are required to take and pass a test ascertaining their knowledge of health and safety precautions, as well as the current state regulations. Performing a tattoo in Oregon State without a proper and current license or in an unlicensed facility is considered a felony offense.[3] Tattooing was legalized in New York City, Massachusetts, South Carolina and Oklahoma between 2002 and 2006.[4]

Pantera – **Pantera** was an American heavy metal band from Arlington, Texas. The group was formed in 1981 by the Abbott brothers – drummer Vinnie Paul and guitarist Dimebag Darrell – along with vocalist Terry Glaze. Bassist Rex Brown joined the band the following year, replacing the original unofficial bass guitarist Tommy D. Bradford. Having started as a glam metal band, Pantera released four albums during the 1980s. Looking for a new and heavier sound, Pantera replaced Glaze with Phil Anselmo in 1987. With its fifth album, 1990's *Cowboys from Hell*, Pantera introduced a groove metal sound. The sixth album, 1992's *Vulgar Display of Power*, exhibited even heavier sound. *Far Beyond Driven* (1994) debuted at number one on the *Billboard* 200.[1]

Tensions began to surface amongst the band members when Anselmo became addicted to heroin in 1995, which nearly led to his death in 1996 following an overdose. These tensions resulted in the recording sessions for *The Great*

Southern Trendkill (1996) to be held separately. The ongoing tension lasted for another seven years, in which only one studio album, *Reinventing the Steel* (2000), was recorded. Pantera went on hiatus in 2001, but was disbanded by the Abbott brothers in 2003 amid communication problems and their conclusion that Anselmo would not return to the band.

The Abbott brothers went on to form Damageplan, while Anselmo began work on several side projects, including Down in which Rex Brown joined as well. On December 8, 2004, Dimebag Darrell was shot and killed on stage by a deranged fan during a Damageplan concert in Columbus, Ohio, permanently ending hopes for a reunion.

Inspiration – Artistic inspiration, sudden creativity in artistic production.

Expectation – **Expectation** or **Expectations** may refer to: To do or be someone or something in another ones point of view.

All information in glossary section taken from Wikipedia